Dead 1

This edition first published 2016 by Fahrenheit Press

www.Fahrenheit-Press.com

Copyright © Jo Perry 2016

The right of Jo Perry to be identified as the author of this work has been asserted by her in accordance with the Copyright, Designs and Patents Act 1988.

All rights reserved. No part of this publication may be reproduced, stored in a retrieval system, or transmitted in any form, or by any means, electronic, mechanical, photocopying, recording or otherwise, without permission in writing from the publisher.

F 4 E

Dead is Better

By

Jo Perry

Fahrenheit Press

For Tom

"Sometimes dead is better."

Stephen King, Pet Sematary

*"Death is no more than passing from one room into another
But there's a difference for me, you know. Because in that other room I
shall be able to see."*

Helen Keller

Chapter 1

"When the first living thing existed, I was there waiting. When the last living thing dies, my job will be finished. I'll put the chairs on the tables, turn out the lights and lock the universe behind me when I leave."
Neil Gaiman, *The Sandman, Vol. 3: Dream Country*

All I know is that I know. And I can't stop knowing. There was no cinematic replay of my life, no white light, no luminous passage to a perpetual meadow populated by old friends and relatives—I didn't float over my failing body as the life seeped out.

I couldn't see a goddamn thing—my eyes were shut.

There was then—the team of EMTs working on me, one applying compressions to the disco beat of the Bee Gees's "Stayin' Alive," and a small young woman with long, curly hair squeezing the breathing bag attached to a plastic tube they'd shoved down my throat. Then a tall young man with short black hair loads me onto a gurney.

That was that.

Bullet holes still interrupt my flesh. My sternum is cracked, my chest bruised black and purple from their efforts.

One thing about this place—it's come as you were.

Chapter 2

"We do not need to grieve for the dead. Why should we grieve for them? They are now in a place where there is no more shadow, darkness, loneliness, isolation, or pain. They are home."
John O'Donohue, Anam Cara: A Book of Celtic Wisdom

No Virgin Mary Blue sky. No combustible darkness. Just a flash, a bang, and a fade-out that delivered me to this quiet place without midnight or noon, twilight or dawn. This place, if it is a place—a beach without a sea, a desert without sand, an airless sky.

Did I mention the goddamn dog?

For the record, she wasn't mine on the other side—which proves that error is built into the fabric of the universe—if that's where we still are.

No ragged holes singe her gut, and she walks without a limp, but there's a dirty rope around her neck that trails behind her too-thin body covered with long, reddish fur. The first moment I saw her, I could tell—She'd been tethered long enough without water or food to die.

Well, she's not hungry or thirsty now. Is that peace?

Chapter 3

"Whatever can die is beautiful — more beautiful than a unicorn, who lives forever, and who is the most beautiful creature in the world. Do you understand me?"
Peter S. Beagle, The Last Unicorn

In life I'd heard of dogs like her, cheap burglar alarms. Solitary, lonely, they bark at passersby and garbage trucks from behind high fences in exchange for water and kibble when the people remember to feed and water them.

They bark out of fear.

And to remind themselves that they in fact exist.

Now that I think about it, I wasn't much different.

A nobody.

A man of no importance.

On the other side, being a nothing had advantages. People barely saw me and that made me free. I moved among them like a shade, a cipher. And when they did acknowledge whoever they thought I was, they were often revealing, entertaining—overconfident, saying too much about spouses and ex-spouses and email passwords, and what the neighbor's son really did in the garage, and about not really being married, or the time they shoplifted—confessing, boasting.

Being nothing—that's my gift

Chapter 4

"When you're dead, they really fix you up. I hope to hell when I do die somebody has sense enough to just dump me in the river or something. Anything except sticking me in a goddam cemetery. People coming and putting a bunch of flowers on your stomach on Sunday, and all that crap. Who wants flowers when you're dead? Nobody."
J.D. Salinger, The Catcher in the Rye

In case you wondered, yes. When you're dead, you can attend your own funeral. It's not required, but I decided to go—time is unknowable here—to try to find out what happened.

And I thought the dog might like a change of scenery—or any scenery.

I want to look at certain people's faces, especially my own.

Late morning at Mount Sinai, Hollywood Hills—which should be named Travel Town 2.0. The final resting place of thousands of corpses sits next door to Travel Town, a collection of non-traveling train cars frequented by babysitters, little boys and blinking coyotes who venture out at noon, when the picnickers and homeless eat their food.

The ferocious September heat and smog smudges LA's edges and boundaries—until it doesn't seem that different from this place, except that the dog and I are temperature-controlled—perpetually lukewarm, courtesy of Who or What we do not know.

The living—palpable, whole, shiny and fragrant with sweat and irritation—nothing's worse than LA traffic on a Friday afternoon—remind me of those silvery-mirage-pools that form on the surfaces of overheated streets and then evaporate when you get close. Although it was I who lacks presence, they seem insubstantial, like flames, the men in suffocating dark suits and ties, and the women—especially my four exes—lotioned and gleaming, tucked and tanned, manicured and lap-banded, and holding wads of Kleenex in their diamond-ringed left hands to signify their former closeness to and recent repudiation of the deceased, who lay by himself in a plain wooden box up front.

The dog, whose rope I hold in my right hand, urges me forward, and then waits patiently while I look.

Jesus. Why is the casket open? I look like shit. I must have Mark's wife "the decorator" to thank for this grotesque violation. Why didn't they shut the box as is customary, especially here in a Jewish place. What were they trying to prove? That despite being shot to death I was still in some sense, intact?

Was I ever really the poor fuck who lived behind that face? The neck and chin have been painted with peach make-up, and the too-pink lip-glossed mouth forced into a grimace that was, I guess, supposed to indicate post-mortal composure. It must have taken three guys at least to wedge my fat ass into the narrow box. I'm large.

Or I was.

I feel strangely light on my feet now. Want to lose sixty pounds in a hurry? Die.

Chapter 5

"Life is a sexually transmitted disease and the mortality rate is one hundred percent."
R.D. Laing

Living people the dog and I saw at my internment:

Mark, my estranged piece of shit brother.

His wife, Helen, self-styled interior decorator.

Former wives and the parasites—my stepchildren—and the wives' boyfriends.

Two plain-clothes police officers with matching salt and pepper mustaches who texted on their cell phones throughout. I've never seen them before.

My accountant.

The office manager, Lena.

My senile neighbor, his wife and daughter-in-law, who must have come because the neighbor can't drive any more.

My hypochondriac cousin Sheila.

My barber, Tony and his ex-wife.

Margarita, my cleaning lady and her son.

Two coyotes.

The rabbi, provided by the cemetery, was a scarecrow of a woman wearing thick brown shoes.

At the gravesite she recited the Kaddish as if she were addressing toddlers, first in Hebrew, and then in English:

Yitgadal v'yitkadash sh'mei raba b'alma di-v'ra chirutei, v'yamlich malchutei b'chayeichon uvyomeichon uvchayei d'chol beit yisrael, ba'agala uvizman kariv, v'im'ru: "amen." Y'hei sh'mei raba m'varach l'alam ul'almei almaya. Yitbarach v'yishtabach, v'yitpa'ar v'yitromam v'yitnaseh, v'yithadar v'yit'aleh v'yit'halal sh'mei d'kud'sha, b'rich hu, l'eila min-kolbirchata v'shirata, tushb'chata v'nechemata da'amiran b'alma, v'im'ru: "amen." Y'hei shlama raba min-sh'maya v'chayim aleinu v'al-kol-yisrael, v'im'ru: "amen." Oseh shalom bimromav, hu ya'aseh shalom aleinu v'al kol-yisrael, v'imru: Amen.

    Glorified and sanctified be God's great name throughout the world, which He has created according to His will. May He establish His kingdom in your lifetime and during your days, and within the life of the entire House of Israel, speedily and soon; and say, Amen. May His great name be blessed forever and to all eternity. Blessed and praised, glorified and exalted, extolled and honored, adored and lauded be the name of the Holy One, blessed be He, beyond all the blessings and hymns, praises and consolations that are ever spoken in the world; and say, Amen. May there be abundant peace from heaven, and life, for us and for all Israel; and say, Amen. He who creates peace in His celestial heights, may He create peace for us and for all Israel; and say, Amen.

Chapter 6

"The hour of departure has arrived, and we go our separate ways, I to die, and you to live. Which of these two is better only God knows."
Socrates

Suffering is finite.

The dog's dry, fissured and muddy paws tell me that in life they touched nothing clean or green, lolls on her back in the freshly-mowed cemetery grass behind my brother, who is the first to take the shovel and drop chunks of the Hollywood Hills ceremoniously upon my casket. I study the backward looks bestowed upon the box under the dirt inside the hole that would have been full of abundant peace but for the angry hiss of Friday traffic on the 134 Freeway. The dog looks at the sky.

I learned some things at my funeral:

The thing about suffering.

That the dog isn't going anywhere.

That my death was "a shock," "terrible," "tragic," but not the details that made it shocking, terrible or tragic.

That I've been dead for 24-48 living hours—Jews must be buried quickly.

I remove the rope from the dog's neck and see where it has worn away the fur.

In the mourners' faces I had detected neither triumph nor grief.

Oh and the cops don't have any idea who killed me.

Chapter 7

"The present life of man upon earth . . . [is] like the swift flight of a sparrow through the mead-hall where you sit at supper in winter . . . The sparrow, flying in at one door and immediately out at another, whilst he is within, is safe from the wintry tempest, but after a short space of fair weather, he immediately vanishes out of your sight, passing from winter to winter again. So this life of man appears for a little while, but of what is to follow or what went before we know nothing at all."
The Venerable Bede, Ecclesiastical History of the English People

The dog and I are outside the hall all right, somewhere between what is, what was and what will be. If you, the living, are the sparrows then the dead are the shadows of your wings.

Did I mention the boyfriends?—The director of development at a private university. The chiropractor/nutritionist who works on the Kardashians. Not the girls. The mother. The pot doctor? The jock who owns gyms? Calling men in their forties and fifties "boyfriends" feels wrong but that's what they are to my four exes.

I'll just say the exes have moved on nicely since the divorces. They live in catshit yellow faux Tuscan villas or fake castles outfitted with bidets, pot fillers, and butler's pantries that require an army of undocumented workers to maintain. Their men have their own exes and stepchildren whom they bring along to cabins in Arrowhead and mid-century modern Palm Springs palaces filled with Jonathan Adler ceramics. They play tennis and golf. They even fucking ski.

My ex-wives, they looked good. As if in shedding me they'd stepped out of fat suits they'd been wearing for a party. Some fucking party.

Chapter 8

> *"The night sky is only a sort of carbon paper,*
> *Blueblack, with the much-poked periods of stars*
> *Letting in the light, peephole after peephole—-*
> *A bonewhite light, like death, behind all things."*
> Sylvia Plath

Here, knowing is free. In life, everything costs.

You're probably wondering why the accountant to a fat-ass nothing like me would drive all the way from Montecito for a Friday afternoon funeral in Glendale. The answer is Happy Andy:

Happy Andy. As in (and feel free to sing along with me):

"Happy Andy, Happy Andy, Oh what fun for you and me!
Happy Andy, he's so Dandy, Oh he never wears a Frown!
Happy Andy, He's so Funny when he Tumbles to the Ground!
Happy Andy is Our Very Very Favorite Rodeo Clown!"

The Happy Andy Show, the most popular kiddie series in the early fifties. Happy Andy lunch boxes and thermoses, Happy Andy plastic Colt .45s and plastic horses, Happy Andrea Cowgirl Dolls. Happy Andy Action Figures, costumes, fringed leather jackets, cowboy hats, then Happy Andy Foods—Happy Andy Pops and Happy Andy Candy (milk chocolate balls with puffed rice and marshmallow centers), and Happy Andy Cereal (milk chocolate balls with puffed wheat and marshmallow centers); Happy Andy Yogurt, Happy Andy frozen Mac & Cheese, Happy Andy Juice Boxes; and Happy Andy Take Anywhere Cheddar Cheese Balls.

The Happy Andy brand has a half-life longer than uranium, emitting money and fueled by the animus of my late manic-depressive, paranoid, stingy, cruel, egomaniacal, man-, woman- and child-hating bastard of a father, Happy fucking Andy, the Jolly Rodeo Clown.

Chapter 9

"We should keep the dead before our eyes and honor them as though still living."
Confucius

Is everyone who dies assigned a companion? I've heard of spirit animals, but there's no way this gentle, graceful, beautiful skinny creature could be meant for someone like me.

The dog sits quietly. I don't mean usually, I mean all the time—if we're somewhere where time matters or exists.

As if something is about to happen.

For all I know we've both been here for centuries, she sitting, me standing next to her, the person or persons who killed me in their own timeless otherworlds. Her calm, sweet brown eyes are open, and she's always looking, though there's nothing to see—at least with my dead eyes. I can tell she's got something she's thinking about or contemplating—a Buddha without a tree, much less a gingko, to piss on.

Could it have been for money that I was killed? There have always been shitloads of Happy Andy bucks to go around—in trust funds, from the buildings on Wilshire, stock, the house and vineyard in Napa, a house in Santa Barbara, the Manhattan apartment, the condos in Scottsdale, the movie theaters. Enough for my father, who wanted to be a mathematician, not a fake rodeo clown with a puppet and a miniature accordion. Enough for the exes, the parasite stepchildren's private schools, tutors, horseback riding lessons and college funds. Enough even for the boyfriends, the pool men, the plastic surgeons, landscapers, decorators and manicurists, personal trainers, private chefs, etc.

Enough for my mother and that snake, my former business partner. Even enough for my brother.

Chapter 10

> *"Everything ends in death, everything. Death is terrible."*
> Leo Tolstoy, *War and Peace*

I need to figure out what happened to me. Maybe that's why I'm here.

I can see before. And I'm up to my ass in the after. But the dying and the arriving here involve information unavailable to me—at least right now. I wonder if it's the same for the dog.

Is she thinking, too, about how she died and when?

As she rests her chin upon her paws, her face is sweet, kind, intelligent, thoughtful, and inscrutable. I suspect she's trying to figure shit out or waiting. But for what? Maybe she's wondering what she did to deserve me.

I discovered that she likes her forehead scratched. Sometimes she rolls over to expose her gaunt belly for a rub. She doesn't seem uncomfortable, but I wish there were a way I could fatten her up.

How long does it take a dog to die without food or water? How long for a man to starve to death? I read that the IRA hunger strikers took 20 or so days to finally die. How long does it take to bleed out, to die from a bullet or from loneliness or failure?

The dog rolls over and holds me in a sad and serious look.

I realize that for her the days are not exactly numbered and that dying must have taken what felt like a very long time. Hunger. Thirst. Then numbing cold and weakness.

And the worst must have been the sensation of being absolutely forgotten and alone.

    I was far luckier in death, I can tell. I'm wearing street clothes, not a hospital gown. My shirt is unbuttoned but I'm wearing one. I think it's safe to assume that my brain didn't go first and it didn't take months or years for the rest of me to go. That's how my mother went and I do not recommend it. My father died all at once, like a flower blooming in reverse, folding back into his then frail self, becoming something small, hard, seed-like, oozing brown urine, fighting for air. All this on the morning of my mother's funeral. You'd think having made her life hell, he'd let her go. But out of malice or habit or some kind of twisted love, he followed.

Chapter 11

"Death is our constant companion, and it is death that gives each person's life its true meaning."
Paulo Coelho, The Pilgrimage

The beautiful dog beside me is dying proof that nothing goes justly, peacefully or kindly. Everything is royally, magnificently, thoroughly fucked up. I'm sure I'm mucking things around right here right now. Not that there are any "things," or any "now," but you know what I mean.

The same force that instills our cells with life makes them cancerous. The qualities that make us love someone, eventually limit them and deaden us. My four failed marriages and abortive "careers" in —real estate, the FM Jazz station (KBop), the dating service for atheists and being Senior Vice-President of AndyCo.—show me that we don't make mistakes—we are mistakes.

Chapter 12

> *"Call no man happy . . . until he is dead"*
> Herodotus

My nothingness became complete the moment I gave in and joined the family business. I was a loser working for his wildly successful father, then, for his brilliant older brother.

If it wasn't for money that I was murdered, then why? Resentment?

Why go to the trouble of killing a failure, a nothing?

Above us jets roar in and out of LAX. If we were visible, we'd be shadows blurring the entrance to AndyCo.'s "world headquarters"—not a total joke, but come on—the "world" seems unaware of this nondescript silvery low rise that seems, in early morning haze, to be constructed of blocks of smoggy sky instead of glass and steel. Out of nowhere a skateboarder with his baseball cap on backwards and wearing a backpack and iPod ear buds clatters right through us, producing in me the tiniest of tiny shivers—but does not interrupt the dog's composure. She's like a still pool into which you can throw stones as long as you want—no ripples.

Look where you're going, asshole, I yell. Fuck you!

He doesn't hear me.

Shit. That guy would have killed us if we'd been alive.

We are not blobs of ectoplasm that float around the living like spectral jellyfish. We are something else, maybe something electromagnetical—that's what it feels like, anyway. Whatever thought or pain is made of—that is what we seem to be. Still, I wish there were some grass for the dog. There isn't. Just those lunar white landscape rocks piled around the elephant-skin trunks of three anemic palms. There are gum wrappers and cigarette wrappers on the rocks, even a crust of hot dog bun. The dog ignores them.

The dog looks in the direction of the parking lot entrance. My brother Mark arrives in his black Ferrari, and straddling the parking space marked "Reserved for President M. Stone" and the one next to it, ("Reserved for Vice President C. Stone" —that's me, Charles Stone) occupying both. I watch him pull his tall self in skinny jeans and dark shirt (My mother was slender and tall, my father was short and fat. I'm sure you can guess by now which one I resembled.) from the sleek, low vehicle, then reach in to grab his bottle of SmartWater and a briefcase. He walks gracefully, on the balls of his feet—he has his own Bikram Yoga studio built into his home in Benedict Canyon—to the glass door, unlocks it, and steps inside the building.

A moment later blue Nissan Leaf pulls into the lot and parks two spaces over. A young African American woman in a linen black pantsuit and shiny blow-dried brown hair gets out. Don't know her. She also has a briefcase, but hers is on wheels. She follows Mark inside. The dog trots to the middle of the parking lot, lies down and shuts her eyes. I follow, then stand next to her wondering if Lena and the others will soon arrive.

I suppose we should go in, but I fucking hate this place. How many times have I pulled into this lot and just sat inside my car, eating Randy's doughnuts and drinking Randy's Donuts coffee, trying to talk myself into going? I remember feeling that I'd rather die than walk through the door. Now that I'm dead you'd think I wouldn't find myself outside again. There's an unsatisfying symmetry to my situation.

Then I notice the Leaf's license plate.

Chapter 13

"Death is just another path, one that we all must take. The grey rain-curtain of this world rolls back, and all turns to silver glass, and then you see it."
J.R.R. Tolkien

"MuCorp213."

Why am I surprised that this would happen so soon after my tragic and shocking exit—if I'm reading time correctly?

When was I, excuse the expression, "laid to rest"? Yesterday?

That means Mark's taking a meeting with that woman from MultiCorp on the Saturday after my funeral. And no one else from the office or the family is here.

MultiCorp, in case you've been living in a cave somewhere, is a kraken that eats little companies like AndyCo. like krill. MultiCorp. is a monster—producing drugs, cosmetics, vaccines, petroleum, and hotel, hospital and stadium "hospitality products and foods." MC has wanted the Happy Andy Brand and AndyCo. for at least two years, but I, to the frustration of my brother, told MultiCorp. to fuck off, and refused to sell the business that brought me so much misery. Why? Because I could. Because stopping this deal gave me, for the first time in my life, some power.

And there were other reasons, too.

Chapter 14

"I mean, they say you die twice. One time when you stop breathing and a second time, a bit later on, when somebody says your name for the last time."
Banksy

The dog follows the woman to the building entrance. I follow the dog. The woman goes in through the unlocked front door. The dog passes right through the large plate glass window to its left, then, after a moment's hesitation, I do, too.

The sensation of the window passing through me—or is it I who is moving through the glass?—is something like—but not quite, since I can't feel anything here—passing through a freezer—the ghost of a shiver of sharp cold on my face, my hands and especially, my feet.

I'm glad Mark and the woman can't see me. I look literally like death. Like crap. My shirt is bloodstained and torn, and below the bottom of my khakis, my feet are bare. I'm still balding and fat. And, I see it now—there's a hospital bracelet on my left wrist. At least I don't look like that schmuck in the casket yesterday in his navy blue suit, a tallis, and vintage Happy Andy tie.

I stop to look at the huge sepia framed photograph of a grinning Happy Andy riding a spotted pony, and above it a large sign red neon sign that says AndyCo. The other walls contain displays of original Happy Andy memorabilia—lunch boxes, plastic guns, salt and pepper shakers, dolls—in all their iterations. The couch, like everything except the espresso machine, is, according to the interior decorator (Mark's wife) "pristine mid-century modern—an homage to the era in which Happy Andy flourished."

Then the espresso machine growls and sings, mixing with the voices coming from Mark's office.

My shit brother Mark, or I should say, AndyCo. via my shit brother's wife, spent $679.00 plus tax and shipping on this Krupps machine with a Burr Grinder. Only the top of the fucking line for the President and CEO of AndyCo. I won't even talk about the coffee beans Mark has delivered. Since when is Intelligensia Coffee not good enough? No, he gets the beans flown in from the Dominican Republic. And the special soy milk from San Francisco. And the green tea from Burma. And the organic, sustainable vegan lunches from a chef in Santa Monica. The wheatgrass and juices from Malibu. Mark wants to the sweating and "healthy" Yoga King of all he surveys.

The dog walks towards the voice on the thick fifties shag carpet but leaves no paw prints. I walk–but feel as if I'm on an invisible Segue—effortless, weightless. This is nothing like flying, or what I imagine flight would be.

This world is frictionless.

"MultiCorp is absolutely committed to honoring your father's legacy," the woman is saying. I can hear it in her voice that she is smiling, before I can see her doing it.

I stand right behind her, so close I wonder if the tiny hairs on her neck are on end. The dog lies down behind Mark, who sits in a vintage Plexiglas chair behind his Eames teak desk upon which rest two Bauer pottery espresso cups––one turquoise, one egg yolk yellow. Mark is leaning forward now, resting his elbows on the desk, his head on his clasped hands, rapt, and nodding eagerly.

"MultiCorp will assure your father's immortality. And, Mr. Stone, your ongoing creativity and vision will ensure that the Happy Andy brand not only lives forever, but that it thrives."

She emphasizes "thrives." She smiles some more.

You'd think Mark been told that he'd live for fucking ever, he looks so thrilled and happy. "I'm just sorry we had to wait so long to complete this."

The woman parts her lips more widely revealing the pink gums above Lumineered teeth, and pushes a sheaf of papers, out of which little Post It flags in red, green and blue emerge at various locations, across the desk to Mark.

"MultiCorp appreciates your follow-through during such a painful time, Mr. Stone."

Mark pulls the papers close to his chest, as if to embrace them, then attempts a wistful smile.

"Yes. We are all in total shock at the loss of my brother. Especially because of the unfortunate circumstances."

What circumstances? Tell me, I command them both silently. But Mark trails off. The woman nods sympathetically. The hairs on her neck are just fine, thank you.

"I'm sure you all are struggling to deal with this tragedy," the woman says, fiddling with her rolling briefcase. "Please know that you and yours are now part of the MultiCorp Family. MultiCorp mourns with you."

So much for my will, my psychic mojo, my ability to haunt. These two live bodies completely ignore my willed commands.

She stands, and holds a business card toward Mark, "If there is anything we can do, just let me know. My personal line is right here on the card. Don't hesitate to call me."

Mark stands too and accepts the business card gratefully.

The dog stretches lazily, glances back at me, then leaps right through the large glass window behind Mark's chair, as calmly as a bird alighting from a tree. I float, as quickly as I can—I'm still not used to being dead—through the woman, her chair, the Eames desk, the espresso cups, and my brother.

As I pass through them, I hope they feel a momentary sense of dread, and some really hardcore intimations of mortality.

Chapter 15

"Death doesn't exist. It never did, it never will. But we've drawn so many pictures of it, so many years, trying to pin it down, comprehend it, we've got to thinking of it as an entity, strangely alive and greedy. All it is, however, is a stopped watch, a loss, an end, a darkness. Nothing."
Ray Bradbury, Something Wicked This Way Comes

Why wouldn't I sell? I hated the business and my family, so you're thinking, why obstruct the deal with MultiCorp?

To spite my brother and the rest, yes. But it's not that simple.

I had to stand up for something. Once in my life.

I know. I sound like a fucking Boy Scout, which by the way I never was. I was an Indian Guide until the day my father came to entertain our tribe. Another story, but I'll you can guess how it went. Jewish cowboy clowns and Indians don't mix.

The dog rolls over for a stomach rub and as I oblige her, I get the urge to take a last look at my apartment.

Chapter 16

> *"The meaning of life is that it stops."*
> *Franz Kafka*

Welcome to Hollywood, home of the desperate, the deluded, the strung out, the runaway, and, despite the new high rises—like Shearer always says about Santa Monica on his radio show—the homeless. Right now the dog and I drift a few inches above the north side of Hollywood Boulevard between Cahuenga and Vine. It's late afternoon. My apartment is a few blocks away.

Then I see that that the dog is floating above Lassie's star on the "Walk of Fame." Jesus. This dead dog has quite the sense of humor. I wish I had a camera, though I suspect all it would capture would be a ripple in the empty air above the dirty sidewalk.

The dog drifts again, and we float around the corner of Las Palmas until we reach my first-floor apartment in an old orange brick three-story building with prominent fire escapes, a.k.a. the "shithole" to my family. I moved in after college at UCSB and never let it go, even through the four marriages.

103 in stained brass numbers.

No police tape. But there is a what L.A. television reporters like to call a "makeshift shrine" by the "Go Away" doormat under the scuffed door, three burned-out Jesus candles, and a couple bunches of wilted supermarket flowers. Must be from the neighbors—I'm touched.

This time it is I who passes through the door first. The dog follows. There is no chill as we pass through the cheap wooden door, just a momentary intensifying of its darkness. Inside the studio apartment, things appear as they did when I occupied it—brick and board bookcases floor to ceiling stuffed with books—I hate to admit it but I was an English major at UCSB—record albums (folk and jazz) and Happy Andy souvenirs. The dog stretches above the cracked brown leather couch and follows my gaze as I survey what used to be my world: the scuffed wooden floor is covered with books, record albums, boxes, piles of LA Weeklies, LA Times, yellowed, disintegrating copies of the LA Free Press for which, briefly, I reviewed music.

I see that mail has been pushed through the front door slot: A Daedalus Books catalogue. A New Yorker. A Rolling Stone. A letter with a Mexico City postmark from Josue Delores addressed to Señor C. Stone from Solar Textil, Mexico City.

How I wish I had the living sinews that would allow me to reach down and open that letter, but death is real, not some fucking "Topper" movie—the power of telekinesis does not exist in life or in what follows after—at least so far, death is look but can't touch.

Solar Textil is a factory in Mexico City that manufactures and processes textiles for Happy Andy t-shirts, sweatshirts, tennis shoes and zippered tote bags. Solar Textil is the plant where three months ago an eighteen-year-old sewing machine operator named Luz Rodriguez suffered an "unfortunate underbench shafting accident" as she bent down to retrieve some fabric from the floor.

Unfortunately, Luz's hair became entangled in the moving shaft.

Unfortunately, the force of the shaft pulled Luz off her seat, and down on the floor, dragging her head into the shaft and ripping her scalp from her skull. There was no dead man's switch so the machine kept running, her hair still caught until someone turned off the machine and cut her blood-soaked hair. Josue Delores, plant supervisor, informed me and my shit brother of the accident and also that Luz is brain-damaged and in the care of her mother. I told my shit brother and the others that I was visiting a fat farm, then flew to Mexico City and met with Josue, toured the dismal factory and visited Luz and her mother. I learned that Luz had worked there for $3.50 an hour six days a week. That neither she nor her mother had health insurance. That Luz is the mother of an eighteen-month old son and that her father is blind. Back in L.A., I met with my shit brother and told him about the unfortunate accident that had befallen Luz. Mark had AndyCo.'s lawyer draft a letter that wished Luz a speedy recovery and enclosed a check for $5,000—which her mother could cash only if she signed the attached agreement specifying that AndyCo was in no way responsible for her daughter's injury. I called Alan, my lawyer, and had him draft my own letter informing Luz's mother that they were now the recipients of a monthly stipend from a fund I created by selling some Apple stock. The only catch was that they were not to discuss this money with anyone.

I also did a little poking around: Solar Textil is a subsidiary of Syncro, which is part of Free Textile, which is owned by Clothing International—which is owned by MultiCorp.

Chapter 17

"Thank Heaven! The crisis —The danger, is past, and the lingering illness, is over at last —, and the fever called Living is conquered at last."
Edgar Allan Poe

The dog floats at attention above the couch now. I notice her long, delicate eyelashes in the slices of light passing through dusty old wooden blinds. It drove my mother and Margarita crazy that I wouldn't let anyone come in and clean the place. Looking back, I see now that I was terribly passive aggressive, and what were they? Aggressive aggressive?

We only had Siamese cats with cowboy names growing up because Mark is allergic. I never realized until now how beautiful dogs are, how patient and how graceful.

I look at letter from Mexico City on the floor, the record albums and books and wish I'd written a will leaving the albums to KPFK, the books, including my Anglo-Saxon dictionary, to the West Hollywood library. I'd like to burn the Happy Andy stuff but of course I am unable to light even one small candle to take away this darkness. I look wistfully at my stereo and long to hear a little Fred Neil. It's too quiet, even here, in the world of the living, as if our presence muted sounds. It seems that the dog and I bring our own cool, weightless bubble of quietness with us wherever we go.

I'll be lucky if my shit brother's wife dumps my record collection at the Goodwill. More likely my stuff is destined for the Dumpster out back.

But I'm beyond luck now, good or bad, don't you think?

And unless there are concerts in hell or wherever I am or am destined to go, Goodbye Teddy Wilson. Faretheewell, Fred Neil.

Chapter 18

> *"Death is not the opposite of life, but a part of it."*
> *Haruki Murakami*

We've returned from Hollywood to our little corner of sweet nothingness here in Etherville. I sit cross-legged next to the dog, her head resting on my thigh. We both stare straight ahead into the blank unknown.

She likes her ears scratched, I've learned. So I am scratching the places where the fur looks short and downy. My bare left foot touches her fur—and I still expect it to feel warmth, but of course, the dog and I are no longer warm. But she is soft and that is something. Funny that the tactile sense works here but not in the world of the living.

Death has a physics all its own.

Visiting my apartment told me some things: I wasn't burglarized, then killed by a crazed addict desperate for something he could pawn for drug money—a scenario my family never tired of rehearsing for me, a first-floor resident of a seedy Hollywood flat who possessed neither a gun nor an alarm system.

Chapter 19

> *"Death, in itself, is nothing; but we fear,*
> *To be we know not what, we know not where."*
> *John Dryden*

After my parents died, Mark insisted on selling the house they'd lived in and in which we grew up. Our bedroom walls were covered floor to ceiling with murals picturing scenes from Happy Andy's adventures, painted by studio artists and set designers who'd worked on the show. The kitchen, too, had murals and mosaics of Happy Andy and his pony. There was a large patio with a western style bar, complete with swinging wooden doors. The house was off Laurel Canyon near Mulholland Drive, but on the valley side. In the fifties and sixties its four bedrooms and two baths (and one "powder room" —with lime green and brown wallpaper featuring lassos and cowgirls—) counted as a big fancy house, ranch style of course, a sprawling one story with a large kidney-shaped pool and a guest house out back that became my father's office. The oaks were big and so noisy with mockingbirds and scrub jays, the pool man had to come three times a week.

After the sale, the trees were cut down and the ample lot divided into three narrow lots that now hold three treeless futuristic two-story stucco "residences."

The dog would have liked that house, the large shady and green back yard, although I think that were she to return to life, she'd spend most of her time indoors. Right now she seems content with our deathy peace and to not be suffering—placid, humble, accepting of whatever is.

Chapter 20

> *"Death will be a great relief. No more interviews."*
> Katherine Hepburn

My first wife, Julia is so unlike this dog in character—I was about to say "spirit" but even from this post-mortal vantage point, I still have no fucking idea what soul or spirit could possibly be or mean. Even if I am one or had one.

Which I seriously doubt.

Upon entering death's kingdom, one is not given a mirror or a map. It's just get off your fat ass and muddle the fuck along, just like life.

Still, just to take the comparison to its conclusion, both the dog and my first wife are female, auburn haired, delicate. Both have been my companion—but this silent dead, starved dog is more lovely, interesting and good than that warm, breathing woman could ever pretend to be.

In life, seeing, being around, or recalling my first wife Julia always put me in a black mood, a shitty funk that drove me to my dim apartment where I'd eat—swallowing my anger and humiliation as I swallowed my food—and listen to Tim Buckley—"I Must Have Been Blind"—and Jim Kweskin —"How Can I Miss You If You Won't Go Away?"—The Chambers Brothers and Tim Hardin—and mourn the ratfuck that was our marriage.

The day our marriage died, Julia merely stopped speaking to me. After lunch that same afternoon—I remember it clearly—we ordered in corned beef and pastrami from Junior's—I was served with divorce papers in my AndyCo office—a public humiliation she'd engineered with the help of a lawyer my shit brother Mark had helped her find.

Our marriage was a ratfuck, did I say that? I did not become the person she thought I was going to be: thin, aggressive, important, cool—i.e. I did not become my shit brother.

If I could appear to Julia as, let's say, Hamlet's father appeared to him, literally the walking dead and wounded, still large, disheveled, and puzzled, a skeletal dog at my side —a weird canine Laurel to my Hardy— Julia would be neither impressed nor afraid, just smug and maybe a little bit amused.

For don't the circumstances in which I find myself justify what she thought of me all along?

I was a failure as a living man. And so far I'm one massive fuck up at being dead.

Chapter 21

*"The boundaries which divide Life from Death are shadowy and vague.
Who shall say where one ends and the other begins?"*
Edgar Allan Poe

The dog stretches out on her belly, her back legs extended straight behind her, her front paws under her chin, a foot above Julia's white marble patio—as if to savor the coolness of the stone, but I know this is not possible. Maybe she likes the smooth look of its surface. Or perhaps she is thinking about something else.

Huge bougainvilleas vomit their pink against both sides of the peach-colored three-story faux French castle on a little manicured green hill above Sunset Boulevard from which I hear the traffic's whisper and the angry buzz of nectar-drunk hummingbirds. I hover like a fat puff of steam above the dog.

A short woman in her thirties with coffee-colored skin and wearing a white uniform—Serena—opens the French doors. Julia, my shit brother Mark, Helen, my shit brother's wife, the accountant, my cousin Sheila, and my lawyer walk right through the dog and arrange themselves around the glass table set with silver vases of orange and red and pink and white roses and crystal pitchers of iced tea. They are dressed in light colors, as if for brunch at the beach, not a hot (I know it's hot not because I feel it but because I see Serena dabbing her forehead with a tissue) morning in September.

Julia wears tight very white jeans that, from the rear, reveal a white thong, high heeled sandals that show off sapphire blue nail polish on her toes, and an oversized yellow silk shirt. Her red hair is pinned up in a loose bun and she wears sunglasses with rhinestones set into the rim. My shit brother Mark must have just come from yoga. His leather flip flops make sucking noises on the stone as he passes under me in sleeveless t-shirt and — get this—purple drawstring cotton pants.

The clown gene will, despite everything, express itself.

Chapter 22

> *"Know one knows whether death, which people fear to be the greatest evil, may not be the greatest good."*
> Plato

I try to catch their murmured small talk, but am distracted by the dog, who suddenly ascends onto the slick and crowded surface of the glass table, among the glittering glasses and vases just as a strong and gritty gust arrives from the hilltop, blowing leaves and dust into the pool. If I didn't know better I'd think the dog had something to do with the wind, but that's impossible.

The scene is like a double-exposure: what I realize now are the major stockholders of AndyCo. sitting around an outdoor table with a spectral dog superimposed upon their crystal glasses, flowers, diamond rings, shiny watches—with a dead dog staring right in their faces if they could only see.

"Thank you all for coming," Alan, my lawyer says. "I know a meeting this early on a Monday morning is highly inconvenient, but now's as good a time as ever to go over Charlie's estate and MultiCorp has requested that the papers be signed as soon as possible to expedite the sale of AndyCo."

"Was there anything about Charlie that was convenient?" Julia asks, then laughs.

If it were possible to redden in anger and humiliation, I would, but my deathy pallor is permanent—I haven't the blood required to blush. And Julia has earned her laugh—she's the only one of my ex-wives who received AndyCo. shares in the divorce.

I float closer to Mark, right next to the dog, and the glass table parts for me like butter.

"Charlie's business is pretty straightforward," Alan begins, looking through his file of papers. " I couldn't prevail upon him to make a will, so he died intestate." Supreme dope-smoker Alan, my roommate at UCSB who only wanted to be an actor, instead joined his father's law where his greatest role is to pretend to give a shit about his clients.

Intestate. Mark blinks as this little nugget of information sinks into Julia's brain, and then a frown appears between her slender, manicured red brows. My cousin Sheila takes a sip of iced tea and stares at her watch.

"Because he declared no heirs, Charlie's shares of AndyCo., and of the rental properties and other real estate holdings and family investments all go to Mark, his brother."

Jesus. What a dumb schmuck I was. I didn't expect to die. Not so soon. I am or was only 38 when I left that world and entered this one. And to be honest, I didn't give a fuck. Or enough of one to think about leaving what was mine to KPFK or the UCSB English Department or to have had the energy to try to thwart my shit brother in death as he had thwarted me in life.

Another gust blasts the patio, rattling silverware, blowing loose leaves into the water glasses, and making the shiny green stone earrings tremble beneath Julia's small perfect ears. The dog moves close to my lawyer, almost nose to nose. Luckily she isn't breathing, or he'd feel and smell her gamey, damp, warm breath upon his just-shaved face and wonder if he were about to be kissed or bitten.

The wind is stronger now, and, I can tell from the way the palm trees at the edge of Julia's property are bending, and from the way the living dab their damp faces, hotter. I realize a Santa Ana blowing in from the desert, maybe even Death Valley, that will, before the living day is over, parch these hills and ignite the dreams of sleeping arsonists.

"The 2006 Volvo station wagon and the contents of the apartment at 1826 North Cahuenga also go to Mark."

Someone titters.

"That just leaves the irrevocable trust."

"What trust?" Mark asks. "I never heard about a trust."

Alan moves some papers around and drinks some water, looking tired. "About six months ago Charles established an irrevocable trust, for a single beneficiary—" here Alan squints at the page, "one Senorita Luz Maria of Mexico City."

Mark blinks again, but when he's done, his eyes remain slits.

"Senorita?" Julia asks.

Alan nods.

"How much?" Sheila asks.

Alan looks down for a moment. A small teardrop of sweat travels from his forehead to his chin. "Two hundred grand a year."

The dog's tail is wagging now. If she were palpable, the thumps would be audible against the glass table, the silverware and glasses, even in this wind.

"Godamn his fat dead ass, " Julia shouts, "he must have been fucking her, too!"

Chapter 23

> *"Death is contagious . . ."*
> *Madeleine L'Engle*

A brief silence follows Julia's outburst. Even the wind fails. Mark knows who Luz is but his expression reveals nothing about her or the arrangement I made—without telling him—for her care. My cousin Sheila taps something on the keyboard of her cell phone, and Alan busies himself with distributing pens and papers for the assembled living to sign.

"Please sign and date—month, day, year—with your full name on the sections flagged. You'll see there are 18 pages total and 7 require your signature, but there are four copies. Two for AndyCo. and two for MultiCorp."

The living lift their pens and bend their faces toward the papers as if they have begun a difficult spelling test.

"And one more thing," Alan says, loosening his tie. "As your family representative, I received a call from Detective Lee at LAPD about Charles's fatal uh, incident."

Did he say accident? Or incident? What does "incident" mean?"

Serena enters carrying a tray on which glistening berries, toast triangles, and sweating slabs of butter lay on delicate green china plates. She places the plates on the table and refills empty water classes.

Julia looks at her and says, "Coffee."

"Detective Lee brought up the possibility that a reward posted by the family, a substantial reward, might help the police in their effort to gain information. Someone who knows something might be incentivized to come forward."

"What about the gun?" Sheila asks. "Can't they find fingerprints and other information from the bullets?"

Alan nods but looks at Sheila as if she's a moron.

"Good question Sheila, but unfortunately, bullets don't hold prints. I think you mean casings, but the police didn't find any. Or the gun. The bullets removed from Charles's body were distorted, but according to Detective Lee's partner, Detective Sullivan, they came from revolver. A .32. Six shots at close range."

I hadn't thought about the holes in my gut until now. Six. That's overkill, isn't it? Whoever shot me wanted to make sure I'd never get up again. I study the living faces but their placid self-interested expressions remain opaque.

The dog sails from the table and drifts down onto the lawn like a butterfly or a feather, and then she begins to roll. There is a rustle of papers as the wind and Serena reappear, she with a silver tray holding coffee cups, cream and sugar, the wind with a filthy plastic bag that has risen from the streets far below us and positions itself in the thorny bougainvillea, then flaps around.

"The reward. How much? Five. " My shit brother Mark says—"Five" is statement, not a question.   Alan stands as he gathers the papers into his briefcase. "Fifty. Fifty might shake something loose."

Chapter 24

> *"A thing is not necessarily true because a man dies for it."*
> Oscar Wilde

There is no up or down. No here here. No molten center or electromagnetic north to guide or anchor me or the dog who sits in her watchful pose, her gaze planted firmly on my forehead, where the third eye would be if I had one. Which I'm sure I don't.

Here, there is nothing to see. There is no time to swim with or against. Still I feel the need to unbutton my tattered shirt and to contemplate what once was my navel.

The three ragged and congealed bullet wounds, one in the navel, two other near it, beneath the overhang of my belly, are slits, not circles. There is hair, some crusted blood, some yellow bruising and some threads from my blue shirt along the edges. The three holes in my gut are round with a gray smudge encircling them. What is it? I don't know.

With my index finger I find a hole near my throat, which I, mirror-less, cannot see, but I know is there. When I withdraw it from the cavity, there is the gray material and a few strings of black mucous on my finger.

I wipe my hand on my blood spattered, tattered shirt, then as I am about to stroke the dog's head, she licks my finger clean with her dry, gray tongue.

I've learned:

I wasn't killed in my apartment, at AndyCo or in my car.

My distracted, rich, cousin Sheila didn't shoot me.

Alan, my lawyer, didn't kill me, either. I was of no value to him dead.

I don't think Julia killed me although she's capable of delegating the task to someone else.

And Julia knew that Serena and I were fucking.

My shit brother Mark—I'm not positive but he could have done it. Did the sale to MultiCorp mean that much to him? Or was it spite?

My 38 years of life on earth were an obscene waste of time, space and metabolism, and semen—my own and my father's. Not that I should have procreated. Just that I should have stopped the Bartleby the Scrivener schtick and taken something seriously, all the way. Done something, anything that meant something.   At the moment of my death, my murderer and I stood face to face.

Chapter 25

"Death is not anything... death is not... It's the absence of presence, nothing more... the endless time of never coming back... a gap you can't see, and when the wind blows through it, it makes not sound..."
Tom Stoppard

Welcome to KDeath, where it's all dead folk singers all the time, and every day is Dia de los Muertos!

Good morning, good afternoon and good night!

It's another perfect not exactly cloudy not exactly bright so-called day here in the afterworld!

The dog stands and it is I who sit cross-legged, my bare chubby feet exposed to the fuzzy not-exactly light or darkness.

Wake up and smell the nothingness, I say as the radio DJ inside my head. That last set was Ramblin' Jack Elliott's "Will the Circle Be Unbroken," "Coming into Los Angeles" by Arlo Guthrie, and of course, Fred Neil's "That's The Bag I'm In." Now for Mimi and Richard Farina's "Reflections in a Crystal Wind."

In my current porous condition, I wonder if the dog can hear the sweet, sad voices and dulcimers playing in my mind's ear:

*"If there's a way to say I'm sorry
Perhaps I'll stay another evening
Beside your door, and watch the moon rise
Inside your window, where jewels are falling
And flowers weeping, and strangers laughing
Because you're dreaming that I have gone..."*

Which reminds me of my dulcimer. Yeah. A big ass like me played the dulcimer. Lately it lived on the top shelf inside the tiny coat closet in my apartment in a shiny wine-colored case. I imagine Serena—grieving my absence, lighting a Jesus candle for me, or just philosophically moving on?— and her sister Maria, enlisted for this special job, is tossing the lovely instrument into a Hefty bag right now.

Is there a section of the afterworld reserved for people who died in motorcycle accidents? I'd like to find it and talk with Richard Farina for a while, then visit Mimi wherever those who die of cancer go.

I am not sure if my current digs are permanent, or if the violent nature of my death brought me here, or if this destination is somehow unique to my, or I should say, our situation. The dog, like me, died too soon and at the hands of another. Hands that failed to feed or to nurture her. Does the arc of history really bend toward justice? We are beyond or outside history, I know that, unable to bend sunbeams or to cast a faint shadow.

Shit, I wasn't fully alive when I lived. It makes sense that in death I am equally ineffectual.

The dog stands, and presses her face against my cheek, nudging me from this reverie. We have places to pass through and people to see.

Chapter 26

"Life is a great surprise. I do not see why death should not be an even greater one."
Nabokov

We find ourselves wandering lonely as clouds about two feet above the new LAPD administration building exterior, planted with spiky drought-resistant plants, and fronted by a dark granite rectangular "water feature," we move like ripe cheese through a grater through the slotted brass memorial to LAPD's fallen, then swim through the glass into to the bright interior.

Rose glides ahead of me, her noble head erect, her legs frozen mid-stride like a galloping carousel horse, through men and women in dark uniforms or in polyester business suits, many of the men with mustaches, the facial hairstyle of choice for L. A. cops since I can remember—or maybe since "Magnum P.I." was a hit on television.

Who the fuck is Rose, you wonder? A dead chick hasn't found her way to my exclusive and out-of-the-way residence, has she?

No. I decided to name the dog.

Why name a deceased dog? Why not? She enjoyed receiving a name and she likes "Rose," I can tell. It's possible, too, that Rose may be my companion for eternity, that the world of the dead is it. But even if I have just a few death-miles left to go before I'm finally allowed some goddamn sleep, and our post-terrestrial collaboration is a fluke, the dog deserves to have a name—a dignity withheld from her in life that I can give her now.

If I had been shot to death in my apartment, we'd be haunting the Hollywood division station on Fountain near Wilcox. But the exact location of my last breath is something I must find out if I am ever to learn who did me in and why. And if I don't know how I died, I can't make sense of my dismal, pathetic waste of a fucked-up life—well not make sense of but even begin to understand.

We sail through the light, modern lobby of the new ten-story police administrative office building behind City Hall. The lobby opens to the floor below as if it were a concert hall, not a structure built to shelter those who Serve and Protect the living from homicidal drug-crazed criminals. Rose and I float straight up, I below her belly, as if we were stacked inside an invisible and silent elevator, to floor five, just as my lawyer Alan, looking weary in a gray suit and black shirt and tie, emerges from a real elevator, across from which a sign that says "5th Floor Robbery Homicide Division." Alan pauses to consult a business card that he carries in one hand, the other holding the briefcase he had at Julia's, then walks to the third door and enters.

I figure Alan is here to meet with the police officers about my murder because my shit brother Mark is too busy doing what? Striving to make Happy Andy board shorts— hecho en Mexico– immortal for MultiCorp.? Or this could be the day Mark meets with his private Pilates instructor or with his psychotherapist or his—get this—life coach? If anyone could use a coach it's me, a goddamn death coach who could help me make unliving all that it can possibly be for me and for Rose.

Rose has alighted above the linoleum floor, and curls up like a cat, chin on paws, eyes half closed. I know she's watching and listening and thinking seriously about something, so I leave her the fuck alone and float close to, almost on top of Alan as he shakes hands, one then the other, with the men I saw at my funeral. Detectives Lee and Sullivan, I assume, and takes an envelope from his briefcase.

Does Alan feel my proximity, his closeness to the poster boy for dissolution? For extinction? He involuntarily brushes something—me? A shadow? A mote of dust?—from his face, then chugs right along in smooth lawyerly fashion.

"Thank you for seeing me on such short notice," he says.

"Anything we can do to expedite a homicide investigation, we are committed to do," announces the detective in a lightweight gray suit and blue and red striped tie, either Lee or Sullivan. Both wear ID tags with the LAPD badge crest and small printing from lanyards around their sturdy necks, but without my glasses (I haven't seen them since I died—where are they?), for the death of me I cannot read the print. The other man wears a slightly darker gray suit with a solid navy blue tie Donald Trump style shiny tie.

Both are clean-shaven and in their forties. One has short gray hair; the other is bald with a shaved head. The bodies of both are smooth and fit under their clothes, with the bulges of identical ankle holsters visible through the legs of their trousers.

"Mr. Stone's family is eager to offer a reward for information about his murder. I have a check here for you to give to anyone who comes forward with something you can really use." Baldy takes the oversized business check, then hands it to Hairy, who glances at it and then places it on his desk. The room is filled with large desks and telephones. There are bulletin boards on the walls with pictures of faces —I'm not clear if they are victims or suspects, but I guess both—mostly male but some women—all hideous, scared, some of them with scrappy beards, bad skin and unbrushed hair—as if they were roughly awakened from sleep—all frowning and photographed in very bad light with a really crappy camera.

"Fifty grand. Are you sure they want to offer this much? There's no guarantee that even good information will solve the case. Especially this kind of homicide."

What kind? What fucking kind? I wait for an answer but Hairy doesn't elaborate. Six shots is violent, yes, but not extraordinary, is it? And not difficult for a single shooter to accomplish. What was so different about my death? It couldn't have been the victim, me, a nothing.

"Absolutely," Alan says. "The family, AndyCo. and its sister company MultiCorp. have joined together to make this reward substantial in order to show how serious they are about finding justice for Charles Stone."

I get it now. The reward money isn't about the murder. It's business, a chance to announce and advertise and, to use one of my shit brother's favorite words—"monetize"— the merger basically for free. How clever of somebody to use the occasion of my untimely death as a public relations opportunity—I nominate His Shitiness himself, the first born Happy Andy son, Mark Stone and the little lady in the Nissan Leaf.

Rose has uncurled herself and moseyed over to photos of the "LAPD's Ten Most Wanted Gang Members," all sour-looking fellows, many with thin moustaches, and all in white t-shirts with "Name, Gang and Moniker" listed under their faces, many with what look like homemade tattoos on their necks.

I float close to read them: "Fernando Monterey, Crazy Riders Gang, Popeye; Carlos Benitez, The Magician Club; Dude; Leon Martinez; Paca Trece; Flash . . .The names of some of the gangs sound like nice restaurants or sections of Disneyland: Toonerville; Cuatro Flatz, Avenuse; 38th Street, but these fellows are wanted for murder, attempted murder and murder of a police officer. Under each picture is a warning printed in bold red ink:

"WARNING: THIS INDIVIDUAL IS CONSIDERED ARMED AND DANGEROUS. DO NOT ATTEMPT TO APPREHEND SUSPECT YOURSELF. IF SEEN, CONTACT YOUR LOCAL POLICE STATION ASAP."

"We'll coordinate with LAPD Public Relations and let you know when the news conference can be facilitated," Baldy, says.

"Thank you," says Alan, readying to go. "I know the family thanks you for your efforts to date. Also, they would all like to be present at the news conference if that is possible."

"That's fine." Hairy offers, " But let them know that to be useful, it should happen in the next day or two."

Chapter 27

"As death, when we come to consider it closely, is the true goal of our existence. I have formed during the last few years such close relations with this best and truest friend of mankind, that his image is not only no longer terrifying to me, but is very soothing and consoling! I thank my God for graciously granting me the opportunity of learning that death is the key which unlocks the door to our true happiness."
Wolfgang Amadeus Mozart

As Happy Andy used to say, Yippee. Wise, ironic Rose has mastered a trick, or at least revealed a trick she already knew, to me.

After decamping from the fifth floor of the LAPD administration building, I lead Rose around to the west side of the building, looking for grass. Instead we find brown patches of dehydrated sod and dirt over which tall, dusty palms stand guard. Rose wafts over to the place where grass should have been, as quiet and graceful as smoke, but instead of rolling, flips on her back and floats, legs and feet straight in the air, and gives me a sidelong look.

Rose is playing dead.

Once I get the joke, I laugh. A disembodied laugh, but still it's laugh enough to shake my punctured belly, and had I breath, would be enough to whistle through the bullet hole in   my   neck   like   steam   from   a   teakettle.

Chapter 28

"We do not die because we have to die; we die because one day, and not so long ago, our consciousness was forced to deem it necessary."
Antonin Artaud

Strange that Rose and I would find ourselves across the street from one of my haunts in life, Roscoe's House of Chicken & Waffles on Gower in Hollywood. My regular thing was #3, Herb's Special "1/2 Chix prepared country style with two waffles," with coffee and Sweet Netta Ta Ta––sweet potato––Pie and maybe a side of smothered mashed potatoes or grits. Two little perfect domes of whipped butter always perched on the light, crisp, slightly cinnamony waffles like tiny breasts. Two small containers of maple syrup, one for each waffle, rested on the plate near the perfectly crisped and golden chicken. Absofuckinglutely perfect. Often more perfect than fucking, which is another problem I'd rather not go into now.

But it's really too bad the good and beautiful in-life-food-and drink-starved Rose can't have a taste or even a meal of what Roscoe's has to offer, but she, like me, is wholly indifferent to food or any other corporeal pleasure. We're neither ravenous nor sated—just completely emptied of need—and noting the irony of being here bodiless, precisely here, hovering above the two red benches in front of Roscoe's rough wooden exterior.

Three local TV news vans arrive, two plain-wrap police cars, then my shit brother Mark's Ferrari, the Nissan Leaf, and Mark's wife's Helen's white Range Rover—which takes a handicapped space. Mark is in a suit, the one he wore to my funeral.

Helen—so thin the bones in her chest are prominent under her platinum and diamond necklace, wears a tight stretchy black dress, high black heels with bright red soles. Her white blonde hair stays put, as if permanently blown back from her too-smooth, too sunscreened photo-facialed Botoxed forehead. She applies pale, shiny lipstick as men emerge from the news vans' sliding doors and uncoil cable, lights and microphones on stands. They're dressed in shirts and jeans—it must still be hot. I recognize Melanie Vann from Channel 8 and Rob Roberts from Channel 3. Both are much thinner than they looked on television, and orange because of the thick foundation on their faces.

Hairy and Baldy throw open the doors of their car, nod to my shit brother Mark and Helen, then talk for a moment on their cell phones, before joining the reporters on the sidewalk and a police officer in uniform who carries some papers. Hairy and Baldy wear graphite gray suits today and their mustaches are neatly trimmed. Alan appears from around the corner—I don't see his car. He's wearing a black suit, black tie and wrap around shades. He looks like a large Jewish crow.

Although the dog and I could mingle with this gathering of souls, we hang back, like shrouds undulating in an underworldly wind. Usually in the world of the living Rose does her own thing while I do mine, but this time she floats right at my side, looking where I look. It is so strange to see these living people congregated here, where I in life so often felt so empty, so full and so completely alone.

Chapter 29

"While I thought that I was learning how to live, I have been learning how to die."
Leonardo da Vinci

The uniformed officer taps the microphone and blinks in the very white lights. The red lights on the video cameras go on.

"Hello? Can everybody hear me? My name is Officer Harris, Leon Harris, from LAPD Public Relations."

Rob Roberts, holding a notepad and pen, interrupts and says, "Can you please spell your name?"

"Harris. H-A-R-R-I-S L-E-O-N. We are gathered here today with Los Angeles Police Department Detectives Sullivan and Lee, to make an announcement in connection with the shocking unsolved murder of Mr. Charles Stone, 38, right here on Gower Street in Hollywood. The victim's family along with the AndyCo. and MultiCorp companies have donated a $50,000 reward, which they hope will help LAPD detectives solve this baffling and very tragic case."

Here? I was killed here? You could knock me down with a feather if there were any of me left to knock.

Perhaps a waffle-thief high on crack shot me for my wallet or my doggie bag of a chicken thigh and extra waffle? Did I stupidly resist, clutching the greasy bag to my thick chest as he shot me?

The officer hands Baldy the mic, "On Saturday, September 29 about 8:05 p.m. Mr. Charles Stone was murdered as he left Roscoe's House of Chicken & Waffles and was proceeding north on foot on Gower Street, we assume toward his residence on north Cahuenga Boulevard.

According to a studio security guard walking south on Gower, a large group of bicyclists appeared, riding in the street and on the sidewalks, traveling at high speed in the direction of Mr. Stone. The guard says he heard a man's voice perhaps, but he's not sure, saying 'Slow down" or something to that effect. Then the guard reports hearing shots, which we believe were the result of one or more suspects shooting the victim at close range.

"At present we believe the suspect or suspects responsible for this homicidal bike rage incident then exited the scene on their bicycles, leaving Mr. Stone fatally struck from gunshot wounds to the neck and chest. Mr. Stone was pronounced dead at Maimonides Medical Center at 9:08 P.M."

Chapter 30

> *"There is a remedy for everything; it is called death."*
> *Portuguese proverb*

"Bike rage"? You're shitting me. Some angry guy or guys on bikes shot me?

Jesus fucking Christ.

I know the "bicyclists" the cop is talking about—though not personally—and "bicyclists" is too polite a word for these riders who commandeer the streets at night—hundreds at a time running red lights, even riding the freeways to protest what they call L.A.'s "car culture." I've seen them on Cahuenga on their way to Griffith Park.

Assholes. They used to congregate at the Pioneer Chicken in Silver Lake—once another favorite chicken place of mine. Now they're everywhere, especially late on weekend nights. There have been ugly incidents with drivers, brawls and accidents.

I'd sit down on the red bench now if I could. Instead, like a pathetic fallacy, I merely sink—right through the red bench until I am a few inches from the red and white "bricks" painted on the ground, the dog—apparently unsurprised or unmoved at the modus operandi of my demise—smoothly descends beside me.

"This homicide has been particularly troubling for detectives and for Mr. Stone's family members," Baldy goes on. "There have been few leads. Mr. Stone had no gang affiliations or criminal history. So far, with the exception of the security guard, no eyewitnesses have come forward, and we have pretty much exhausted our leads."

The woman from MultiCorp looks terribly sad. My shit brother Mark and his wife assume serious expressions. My lawyer Alan looks at his shoes.

Now it's Hairy's turn: "Anyone with information about this incident should contact LAPD Robbery Homicide Division Detectives Sullivan or Lee. Anyone wishing to remain anonymous should call Crime Stoppers at 1-555-5TIPS. Tipsters may also contact Crime Stoppers by texting. All text messages should begin with the letters LAPDHOM.'"

Chapter 31

"People do not die for us immediately, but remain bathed in a sort of aura of life which bears no relation to true immortality but through which they continue to occupy our thoughts in the same way as when they were alive. It is as though they were traveling abroad."
Marcel Proust

Good luck with the tips, Baldy and Harry and Harris, Leon—fifty Happy Andy grand or not.

I realize now that the meaning I have been searching for—the point of my death—doesn't exist and never will.

My death was accidental. Haphazard. Impersonal.

It doesn't matter into which man's face I shouted—as he tried to run me off the sidewalk with his bicycle, then pulled a gun from—what? His ass? Or as he shot me from his 10-speed?

And you can bet your mustaches I did not yell "slow down." It wouldn't have been me without shouting Fuck off, Drop Dead, Asshole or Blow it Out Your Ass.

The dog and I are back inside this smooth, blurry kingdom of quietness like fetuses adrift in amniotic fluid or crystals inside a geode's darkness. We both stare straight ahead, the dog lying on her side, her eyes open. I sit in a heap beside her, absentmindedly scratching the fur on her bony forehead.

Having learned the circumstances of my death, I am as disconcerted and chagrined as I was before I discovered the truth.

My death lacks meaning. It required nothing of me.

I realize now that my hopes for my death were grandiose. I really wanted something much more than this. A crime of passion directed at me might have burnished my life with real importance.

Instead my death is the punch line of a not very funny joke.

Why did the fat man cross the road?

I didn't expect the flamboyant. No way did I expect that I would go out auto-erotically in Thailand, or during an orgy, or would be ritually stabbed, my body posed like a broken doll by a soon-to-be-famous serial killer.

I suppose the violence of my exit bestows upon it a tinge of noir—but a murderer who doesn't even drive a car, and the homey smells of maple syrup and fried chicken in the air —bring it down to the level of I told you so.

I can hear my shit brother Mark's voice in my head—I told you you were fat. I told you to go on a diet. Why don't you get the fucking Lap Band? Or a gastric bypass? Or get a personal trainer? If you didn't eat so much, you would have been home—in a house with a wife, not alone in your shithole apartment—or at the gym—instead walking home from Roscoe's with a To Go order in your hand—your fat ass and fat mouth in the wrong place at the wrong time.

As usual I got everything wrong. Everything ass-backwards.

And that, boys and girls—as Happy Andy used to say at each show's end—is howdy do—and fucking it.

Chapter 32

> *"Life is pleasant. Death is peaceful. It's the transition that's troublesome."*
> Marcel Proust

Even by otherworldly standards, I have lost track, of no—time—we're beyond time—but what it feels like is that time has lost track of me.

And Rose.

She rolls over for a tummy rub, then stands and looks straight at me. I'm lying on my back, my hands behind my head, as if I'm watching clouds pass above me in a fall blue sky, except there are no clouds, no sky, no up or down, no nothing except nothing, no change in this our little patch of netherworld.

What? What can she possibly be thinking? We know what happened to me now. Mr. Charles Stone died because he couldn't for once in his life stop eating, shut the fuck up or get out of the fucking way.

Rose nudges my left arm with her nose.

I pull my arm from behind my head and sit up. She comes close, bends down, and nudges my wrist.

I pat her head obligingly, and scratch that place behind her ears that she likes scratched.

She sits down on my left, then with her nose pushes the bloodied hospital I.D. bracelet on my wrist.

I look at her expectant, wise eyes.

The bracelet.

I can't get it off, and without my glasses it's tough to even read the words printed on the plastic, but if I hold it close to my eyes, I can read a date—my death day—and my name, my date of birth, my address—the Cahuenga apartment—and the name of a doctor I do not know—Dr. E. Miller— followed by an 8 digit number and the words, "Maimonides Medical Center."

Perhaps Dr. Miller was in the ER and pronounced me dead.

Rose nudges me again with her muzzle, and her usually placid expression is almost impatient.

What can she possibly want? As my mother used to say, when it comes to sex, human anatomy, fetal development, politics and religion, there's such a thing as too much information. And I agree, especially about my own demise. I know more than enough, thank you.

Bike rage is all I had to hear.

I don't think I need to know the name of the bicyclist. And even if I did know who he was, there is no way that I, in my current condition, could exact revenge or effect justice. Or that it, from my new point of view, would matter if I did.

Rose looks at me, her expression fixed and serious. Her brown pupils darkening with intensity, her mouth slightly open.

What can it be? I move my hand to that place along her back that she can't reach but often likes me to scratch, but she moves aside. That's not what she wants at all.

The hospital.

Chapter 33

"Death is for many of us the gate of hell; but we are inside on the way out, not outside on the way in."
George Bernard Shaw

Rose floats beside me, her ears cocked, like the RCA dog listening to its master, as if she's waiting for me to announce something— or even better—to do something wise or significant. The two small, dark dots above her eyes, each with a few delicate long dark hairs springing from their centers, contract in an expectant frown.

I have nothing to say and I have no plan. I feel pretty much the way I always did—like shit—having proven as unequal to death as I was to life. If my heart were anything but a piece of meat, it would be contracting now in spasms of shame and regret.

Perhaps this is why I follow Rose's lead and return to the place on earth where I exhaled my last, pathetic breath.

For the living it's a Tuesday evening in the Memorial Medical Center in West Hollywood—a hospital famous for its studio head and celebrity benefactors and for patients who enjoy four-star meals and in luxurious private suites on its exclusive 8th floor.

My mother died in one of those suites. So did that famous child actor from a heroin overdose, and that 102 year old song and dance girl from the thirties whose last young husband—there were ten—is rumored to have poisoned her tea.

I'm looking for Dr. Miller, the name on my ID bracelet. That's why we drift—like plumes of smoke from a funeral pyre— across the floor well-scrubbed floor of what is known as "the ER to the stars."

The plastic rows of seats in the waiting area are half full—a big black and white clock tells me it's still early—7 p.m. We see no stars, not even one aging-trophy wife or B-list leading man.

There's a pregnant woman in a bright green sari—I'd guess she's thirty—gasping every few minutes and gripping the sides of her chair as her labor intensifies. Her husband, wearing shorts and flip-flops, speaks in Hindi? Urdu? into his smart phone, a large overnight bag at his feet, his eyes fixed on the male nurse sitting at a desk behind a closed glass window over which is a large sign that says EMERGENCY.

We see an elderly couple both dressed too warmly for LA in September in matching wine-colored cardigans. The white haired woman wears her hair pulled back in a ponytail—the hair so thin that large patches of her pink scalp are exposed. Her glasses magnify her very pale blue, very bloodshot eyes. The man seems frail, confused. The woman holds a bloodstained paper towel to his forehead, and now I see that the thin, discolored skin on his elbow is lacerated too. Next to him is an aluminum walker with bright yellow tennis balls stuck on the front wheels.

My survey includes also a 9 or 10 year-old boy in a white karate uniform, sitting sideways, his left leg resting on his mother's lap, a baggy of ice resting on his ankle; a girl in flip flops, and wearing UCLA blue and gold sweatshirt and leggings, her head between her knees and groaning softly; and a well-dressed middle-aged man sitting alone—perhaps waiting for someone inside—or feeling ill in a way his body language won't reveal.

The UCLA girl's friend gets up and walks to the vending machines against the wall. One with sodas and plastic water, one with coffee with a hand-written "Out of Order" sign taped to it, the last filled with snacks and candy. She inserts some coins and returns with a bag of corn chips and a bar of candy, which she eats while her friend pales with pain or nausea. That would have been me—eating was my soporific, my narcotic. Before death and Rose, food was my most reliable and loveliest friend. Especially Happy Andy Take Anywhere Cheddar Cheese Balls—which by the way, one cannot take anywhere—especially not into the other side.

Then the place, excuse the expression, comes alive. The swinging doors of the ambulance entrance fly open and two black-uniformed EMTS, hands in blue latex gloves, trot in pushing a gurney on which Father Time seems to be strapped.

Rose makes a swift turn and glides after them. I follow Rose through the closed electronic door into the treatment area where the EMTs stand at a desk and speak to a middle-aged nurse in dark purple scrubs wearing a pin that says "Nurses <3 Patients." She types on the keyboard of a computer.

The old guy lies with his eyes closed, the gurney pushed against the wall.

"He's 54. Abdominal pain. Intermittent and severe. No fever. BP normal. 130/80," the tall EMT, a young, trim guy with blue eyes and very short-cropped black hair explains.

54? This guy looks 85 at least.

"Address?" the nurse asks.

"Transient."

The man on the gurney groans and the nurse nods toward an empty cubicle. The EMTs push the gurney inside. The narrow space is outfitted with oxygen tubes, monitors on wheels, plastic containers and other equipment whose purpose I do not know, except that if one needs them, it can't be good. Rose and I park ourselves about 4 feet above the patient's bed, right below the fluorescent light fixture, like two empty cartoon bubbles.

Inside the cubicle the EMTs release the straps and slide the man from the gurney onto a narrow bed. The nurse in purple follows, carrying a printout.

"Let's try to make you comfortable—" She looks at the paper, "Mr. Haffer? Jonathan Haffer?"

The man nods, then groans. The nurse's gloved hands unbutton the man's sweat and dirt soiled denim work shirt, pulls a sheet and blanket up to his thin shoulders, then attaches a blood-pressure cuff to the man's bony arm. The man, his eyes open now, returns the nurse's look, but says nothing. I see now that the man is filthy—his chest, neck, face, down to his fingers that end in long, black broken fingernails. His long gray hair is stringy. Dried snot flecks his beard. I suspect that he smells, but my own condition prevents me from confirming this.

A small, beautiful young woman with honey-colored skin, large brown eyes and dark curly hair pulled back into a ponytail, enters the cubicle. She wears a blue t-shirt, blue scrubs and black wooden clogs.

"I'm Doctor Branford," she says to the man and nods at the EMT who smiles. She looks too young, too pretty to be a doctor, but the ID tag around her neck says, "Elizabeth A. Branford, M.D. Emergency Medicine."

Too bad. This is not my Dr. Miller. I wonder about the nurse. Was she with me when I died?

"Where was he picked up?" the doctor asks the EMT as she glances through the printout.

"Downtown. San Julian Street." the nurse smiles wearily.

The other EMT nods. He's also young, but blond and short. "Yeah. The transport was from Wings of Hope."

Wings of Hope—wait, I know that name. It's a Skid Row rescue place for homeless alcoholics and drug addicts. They offer beds, meals, and drug and alcohol counseling. AndyCo. (Really my shit brother Mark) made a tax-deductible donation to it a few months ago, a check for a grand and hundreds of cases of just-expired "product" from the warehouse in Vernon—Happy Andy Candy, Happy Andy Cereal, Happy Andy Yogurt, Happy Andy frozen Mac & Cheese.

Could rotten Happy Andy food have sickened this poor man?

Rose descends, until she's right on the man's chest, then stretches out, her head on his neck, her paws on his shoulders. I expect him to cry out, but if he feels the presence of a dead dog on his chest, he doesn't show it. In fact, his groans subside and the taut muscles in his face relax.

Is Rose trying to tell him something? Or trying to find something out?

The doctor snaps on a pair of beige latex gloves, and bestows a spectacular smile upon the man as she lifts her stethoscope to his chest. "I'm going to listen to your heart, sir."

The doctor slides the stethoscope right through Rose, then presses it gently upon Mr. Haffner's hairless chest, listens, then removes the tubes from her ears.

"Sounds fine," she says and smiles at the man as if she is incredibly happy to be in his company. "Now, Can you show me where it hurts?"

The man points to his gut below the waist.

"Okay. On a scale of one to ten, how would you rate this pain?"

"9."

"I'm going to examine your abdomen so we can find out what's wrong. "

Again, Dr. Branford's hand passes through Rose to expertly palpate the area under the man's waist and abdomen.

"Jesus! Jesus Christ! " the man bellows when she presses the area below his navel.

"I'm sorry," Dr. Branford says.

Rose touches the man's filthy face with her nose, then turns and floats out of the cubicle into the hall. But I'm not done. I want to hear what the doctor has to say. Was it something he ate or not?

"I'll order something for the pain right now." Dr. Branford writes something on the chart, then turns to the nurse.

"Rather than wait around to see if his pain worsens, I'm going to admit. Get him bathed and into a clean gown. Let's start some IV fluids, too."

Dr. Branford turns toward the man whose eyes are closed again, " I'm ordering a C.A.T. scan, blood and urine test, and a toxicology panel for you, sir. So we can find out as soon as possible what's causing the pain in your abdomen."

Then she turns back toward the EMTs and the nurse, "With someone in his situation, there's no way to know what he might have ingested or when."

Chapter 34

> *"Even death has a heart."*
> Markus Zusak, The Book Thief

Rose and I drift inside the blue glow that fills the living world before dawn. I've never known the source of this blue light—is it from the moon or stars? Or outer space? We move above a sidewalk littered with garbage, shopping carts piled high with plastic garbage bags and nylon suitcases, mummy-shapes on the sidewalk covered in blankets and sleeping bags and boxes from which the legs of sleeping human beings extend. A few blocks away, high-rise building, City Hall, the new LAPD administration building and the wing-like Disney Concert Hall begin to shine gold in the emerging sunrise.

In life I avoided—among most unpleasant and difficult things —this place. I banished Skid Row and its people from my thoughts. Sure, every Thanksgiving, Christmas and Mother's Day there'd be a TV news story showing famous actors and actresses wearing aprons and serving a holiday meals on paper plates to a long line of homeless people.

Once in awhile I'd send a check to one "rescue" mission or another. But as I look around, nobody here looks even slightly rescued. A tsunami of bad luck and failure carried these people here on a wave of garbage and debris.

A black and white police car turns the corner, then slows while the officer inside sweeps a flashlight across the inert bodies and detritus along the street and illuminates a crude mural painted on an old brick wall: "Wings of Hope" in thick white cursive over a brown doorway, white angels with pink faces and yellow hair, their wings extended like butterflies, above W and the H.

In smaller letters, "God is Love! All Are Welcome!" is painted in sky blue. I pass through the closed door first, Rose right behind me, into a dark hallway. We pass a small reception area with a desk, a desk chair and about 10 of those white plastic chairs they sell at Rite Aid; a large meeting room with a dry-erase board up front; a small corner room filled with cardboard boxes of shoes, pants, shirts, underwear, and blankets. I see a staircase leading to a second floor. A sign on the landing says, Men's/Women's Dorms.

In the back I find what I am looking for, a large kitchen equipped with a serving station like those in school cafeterias, and long dining tables covered with black and white checked oilcloth and more of those white chairs.

There are no cupboards, just long stainless steel tables and shelves, covered with canned, packaged and boxed foods: jars of mayonnaise and jam, cans of tuna, huge shrink-wrapped packages of spaghetti, bags of bruised onions, oranges, apples, hot dog buns; loaves of bread, packages of cookies, clear bags of doughnuts.

I see no boxes or products with the Happy Andy logo.

Chapter 35

> "... we are all equal in the presence of death."
> Pubilius Syrus

Rose moves from the kitchen area and floats, like a diver slowly ascending to the surface, up the back stairs. I follow, and pass handwritten signs on the landing wall that say "Men's Dorm" with a left-pointing arrow, and "Women's Dorm" with an arrow pointing to the right. Other signs announce "Men's Restroom/Showers," "Women's Restroom/Showers," "No Smoking At Any Time," "No Alcohol, Medications or Controlled Substances Allowed. No Weapons." "Quiet Hours from 9 PM to 7 AM."

A picture of Jesus is taped to the wall at the landing.

We melt through a wall next to the closed door marked "Men's Dorm." Inside, a little light comes from a small street-facing window covered with blinds. The room is crowded with bunk beds and gray metal lockers, stacked one on another. We drift from bed to bed. Most of the men have beards, many with mouths open in sleep, exposing missing, broken or yellowed teeth and emitting snores. There are a few young guys—a handsome man who appears about twenty-five sleeping on his side; a slender young man with his hair dyed purple and tattoos of spiders on his face.

Rose takes me on a tour of the women's dorm as well: A slender, pretty African American woman whose hair is braided in elaborate cornrows lies on her side, awake, clutching a filthy teddy bear. There are women with white hair, brown hair, black hair, auburn hair. One woman so fat her body seems to melt over the edges of the narrow bunk.

Another so small she barely shows under the thin brown army blanket.

A woman about the age my mother would be now sleeps on top of the blankets. She wears just cut off denim shorts, dirty white socks, and a yellow t-shirt that has a picture of a rabbit and the words, "Some Bunny Loves Me." I see movement in the corner on a lower bunk—then realize that there are two bodies under an unzipped sleeping bag, moving up and down.

Chapter 36

> *"Nothing can we call our own but death*
> *And that small model of the barren earth*
> *Which serves as paste and cover to our bones."*
> *Shakespeare, Richard II*

It seems to take for fucking-ever to leave Skid Row. Rose just hangs, and I mean literally, hangs around.

After our fly-by of the dormitories, Rose and I proceed to the alley behind the Wings of Hope. There are three Dumpsters, two padlocked shut, the third one pried open. I look inside. The risen sun's cheery beams illuminate twenty or so dented but unopened cartons of Happy Andy Macaroni & Cheese.

Seeing the boxes in that Dumpster and being back here in our little corner of—could it be Purgatory?—is a relief. But I'm confused. Rose, who was clearly sent here —by what or whom—the Void, God, Nature, Karma, Allah, a subatomic particle or a cosmic joke—to help me solve the riddle of my own demise, is doing a lousy job. I suspect sometimes that our excursions to the other side are entertainment—what an evening or morning walk, or a trip to dog park on the other side would be to a living dog— a dog whose life was nothing at all like hers.

And to make things shittier, Rose interprets my frustration as displeasure. For the first time since our strange postmortal partnership commenced, she lies facing away from me where I sit legs crossed as if I were meditating, which I'm not.

I'm remembering visiting the cemetery (yes, where I am buried, but a different section: "Tradition") with my mother, to place flowers on my grandmother's and grandfather's graves. It must have been about a year after my grandmother died, so I must have been ten. As we walked across the green expanse, I was sure the spring in the grass that I could feel through the soles of my tennis shoes came from the pressure of the dead's skeletal fingers, their long fingernails clawing the earth below me, the hideous struggle going on right below us. But I said nothing.

My mother dropped to her knees before the flat markers, sweeping the leaves and dried grass off with her hand, then stared quietly. Once the flowers had been arranged—red roses from our house— and she was back on her feet, she turned to me and said the weirdest thing: "If you ever need help, Charlie, ask them."

Well I need help, now. The dog and I are lost.

Chapter 37

"There's nowhere else to escape to ... Except in a wooden box, that is."
H.M. Forester, Game of Aeons

Rose drifts in the moonlight like a feather above the dull bronze memorial plaque that reads, "Moishe Burnside, beloved husband, father and grandfather. 1914-1992. Rest in Peace." I hover next to her here with what is left of my grandmother in the living world, a plaque that says, "Ruth Burnside, beloved wife, mother and grandmother. 1916-1995. We will always Love You."

Bubbe, Grandpa, I need your help the voice inside my dead head says.

What am I meant to do? I silently ask, sincerely willing one or both of my dead grandparents to rise from the dark ground and talk to me or just to lie there and talk to me. Or send me a fucking sign.

An otherworldly, high-pitched howl tears through the silence and four glowing yellow eyes appear in the distant darkness, moving right toward me, about two feet from the ground. Rose runs off to meet the eyes as they approach.

But these glowing orbs belong, not to the wise and wraithlike Mr. and Mrs. Moishe Burnside, but to a pair of living, thirsty coyotes who are taking a shortcut from the dry hills through the cemetery down to Forest Lawn Road below.

Chapter 38

"Funerals all over the world everywhere every minute. Shovelling them under by the cartload doublequick. Thousands every hour. Too many in the world."
James Joyce, Ulysses

What I know and don't know after my second visit to the cemetery:

The dead move among the living. Look at Rose. Look at me. That's an expression. I know you can't see me or Rose, but believe me, we are there right with you sometimes.

Unfortunately, I cannot see Rose now. Did she become lost in the world of life or did she choose to remain there? Did she run away? From me? After failing to summon my grandparents, I watched Rose vanish into the night, a graceful shade among shadows, a small silence in a greater one.

I need to find Rose, even if it is just to say goodbye.

And I'd like to know where all the others all are. By others I mean the dead in general, and specifically those I wouldn't mind running into here in the Beyond: my maternal grandparents, Warren Zevon, Christopher Smart, Richard Brautigan, Otis Redding, Anne Frank, John Donne, Richard Feynman, E.B. White, Jim Morrison, Fred Neil, Lenny Bruce, John Keats, Richard Farina, Chaucer, Coleridge, Samuel Johnson, Sam Kinnison, Jesus, Lincoln, Sitting Bull, Einstein. No, not Einstein. Did you know he abandoned his own daughter and treated his sons like shit? I'll take Lord Buckley instead. And some nice dead dogs—for Rose, perhaps—and some dinosaurs for me.

It's like a fucking tomb here it's so quiet, so empty. Hamlet, if he had paid any attention to his ghost father at all, would have known that death, whatever it is, does not involve dreaming. Thinking, yes. And remembering. There's not much to it, really, just the act of knowing and of trying to know, and unrelenting urge to find—okay, I'll say it—the truth.

Expired Happy Andy Macaroni and Cheese wasn't on the menu at Wings of Hope. That means the poor geezer in the ER got sick from something else.

Chapter 39

"On the plus side, death is one of the few things that can be done just as easily lying down."
Woody Allen

I'm back at Memorial Medical Center looking for Rose, for Dr. Miller—for clarity. It's daylight—but I've lost track of the living days. Was I buried two weeks ago, two months? Two years?

Without Rose I am, if this is possible, deader and more alone.

Rose's schtick with my hospital I.D. bracelet brought me here before, but I got sidetracked last time searching for Dr. Miller. Without Rose, I have fewer distractions but less sense of direction. I circulate slowly like bad air through the parking structure, then along the outside of the building, the roof, drifting down, peering into windows.

Inside I check out the exclusive top-floor private suites, float through the locked psych ward, oncology, nephrology, labor and delivery, through labs and operating rooms, waiting areas, nurses' stations, and the ICU. Even the chapel. I've seen the living suffering in a variety of ways, many of them close, very close to death—but no cigar. I found the name "Dr. I. Miller" on a locker in the physicians' changing room and written in blue marker on a dry erase board in Labor and Delivery—but didn't see him—I learned the I is for Ian—and did not find Rose.

All that's left is below ground and the first floor—cafeteria, pharmacy, gift shop, admitting, the ER and a suite of business offices and meeting rooms, security, a laundry, and the basement morgue and pathology lab, where you might expect Rose to be hanging out with a new companion, perhaps the infant I saw wrapped in a small, white sheet.

No Rose.

Just to finish what I started, I scan the people on the hospital's busy first floor from above, looking for Rose's sleek shape, until I'm in an area of carpeted offices and meeting rooms. Color photographs of men in suits shaking hands with well-dressed people dot the beige walls. A secretary in a pants suit sits at a triangular desk at the end of one long hall and speaks on a telephone. Behind her is a closed oak door upon which are shiny raised letters that spell out Frederick R. Nilsson, Chief Financial Officer and through which appears the hazy figure of a dog.

Chapter 40

"Death: The end of life. The cessation of life. (These common definitions of death ultimately depend upon the definition of life, upon which there is no consensus.)"

My reunion with Rose is deeply moving and perplexing. Once we return together to our little corner of the otherworld, she leaps upon me and I embrace her—two flickering gray flames becoming one. The way she licks my pallid face with her dry tongue, you'd think I was the lost soul, not she.

Which leaves me where, exactly?

The doctor who pronounced me dead—I haven't found him yet. The geezer was a dead-end. He had no real connection to me or to AndyCo.

The CFO's office at the hospital, why did Rose park herself there? I've never seen his name before.

Why would Rose run away like that, then return to the hospital, not here?

Why wasn't she looking for me?

What am I missing? What is it that I can't see?

Rose assumes her patient pose again, her wise eyes wide. She reminds me of those small statues of Anubis, dog or jackal, in the British Museum that I liked to visit the summer I was twelve. My father was doing a summer variety show for an English television company. Every morning a car picked him up under the silver pergola of the Savoy Hotel and took him to the Pinewood Studios outside the city. My shit brother and I spent our days wandering London with our mother—and spent time fighting over our stamp collections in our suite overlooking the Thames and Cleopatra's needle.

We returned to the museum often to see the Egyptian art and mummies—not just the humans, but cat and dog mummies too, their painted faces on the mummy cases animated and individual. I still remember a papyrus depicting Anubis with his dog head weighing a dead human heart during a ritual designed to test its purity: The heart, if it proved lighter than a feather, was the soul's ticket into the afterlife. If the heart failed the test, Anubis fed it to Ammit the Devourer.

My own fat, twisted heart should make a nice snack for the Devourer. I look into Rose's sweet and worried face and see in it the expression of a heart purer than Anubis's lightest feather.

What's troubling her?

Rose nudges my hand gently with her nose, as if to urge me to get going, to do something. I have no idea what she wants and before I can stop myself, I pull my hand away, unable to suppress my irritation, my frustration at myself and the absurdity of my situation.

As Rose drops her head and almost cowers, I feel the weight of my own crass self-centeredness.

For most of my life and certainly since my death, I haven't considered anyone except myself.

I pat Rose on the head until her body relaxes.

Stupid, arrogant fuck that I am, the possibility that Rose might have her own concerns—her own unfinished and important business—never occurred to me—not even once.

Because I died or was pronounced dead in the Memorial Medical E.R., I assumed Rose was nudging me toward my own truth.

Well maybe there's truth to be had—but it doesn't belong to me.

And if there's meaning to be sought—it's not located in my own death.

Maybe it's Rose's death that counts.

I look into Rose's expectant and forgiving eyes. As she looks back at me with an expression of love and hope, I could kick myself.

I had everything ass-backwards, I see that now. I was completely mistaken all along.

The dog's not here for me.

I'm here for the dog.

Chapter 41

> *"Death is when the monsters get you."*
> Stephen King

Rose and I circulate inside the spacious office of Frederick R. Nilsson, Chief Financial Officer, Memorial Medical Center, a Medical Corporation. I've spent more time in this fucking hospital dead than I ever did alive, even when my mother was sick with her lengthy final illness.

Mr. Nilsson sits behind a very large desk, slipping papers and printouts into files scattered across his desk, and then shuts down a large desktop computer. He is in his thirties, tall, blond, with very pale blue eyes and slightly sunburned skin, as if he'd spent the weekend wearing sunglasses and water-skiing or playing volleyball at the beach. He wears a dark suit and a tie with a bright sunflower pattern. There is a silver-framed photograph on the desk showing him receiving an award from a gray-haired man in a white coat. A digital clock on the shelf behind him says 7 P.M.

I do not know why Rose has brought me here, but try to be vigilant. I have no idea what to notice or what to look for. I've never seen this perfectly ordinary, dull-looking man before—in my life or since my death.

Nilsson stands, lifts his briefcase to the desk and snaps it closed, then takes a cell phone from his pocket and pushes a button.

"Hi, Mom. I'm leaving now. Need anything?"

Rose and I hear a female voice on the other end, but I can't make out the words.

"Okay. That's good. How was physical therapy today?"

More female sounds, then Nilsson slips his phone back into his pocket, grabs his briefcase and exits the office.

Before I can give Rose a questioning look, she's gliding after him—as if she's a kite for which he holds the very short string—and I follow her through the office door, his secretary's desk, down the hall, up the large elevator, and through the lobby to the parking structure, where he gets inside a white SUV and starts the engine. Along the way he's greeted or been greeted by a variety of people—nurses, janitors, volunteers. He has an easy way about him—friendly, relaxed, warm.

Okay. He's totally—and I mean totally—boring guy, I think. Nice enough, but how can this schmuck be in any way important to Rose?

But Rose isn't finished. She jumps right through the rear door of the SUV into the back seat and looks at me. I slide in beside Rose after the SUV is moving, not difficult in my current condition.

Unaware of his two silent, invisible and weightless passengers, Mr. Nilsson turns on the radio to the country station and, as he drives, up Fairfax past the Farmers Market (one of my favorite places when I was alive, especially Bob's Donuts) sings along loudly to George Jones's "He Stopped Loving Her Today." Not my taste. After a few minutes he swings his car into a narrow driveway of a two-story Spanish style house on Circle Drive. I know where we are—Carthay Circle, a collection of Spanish style homes built around the famous Carthay Circle movie theater in the twenties.

Sprinklers are running on most of the front lawns in the neighborhood in the deepening twilight. The September heat wave must still be going on.

Nilsson parks, takes his briefcase from the front seat and walks quickly to the front door. Rose follows, practically at his ankles. I'm behind Rose.

Nilsson enters a hallway with dark wooden floors. To the right is a living room. At the end of the hallway is a small den or family room. Nilsson goes into the den, but Rose doesn't stop to observe him and sails right over him through some shuttered French doors to the back yard beyond. Once again I follow.

The outdoor area is paved. Two ficus trees grow from large terracotta pots. There's a table with an umbrella and chairs, some lounge chairs, and hand weights in the corner. Rose floats past these things and disappears around a low wooden fence at the very back.

I follow her into a small, treeless area of loose dirt that holds a defunct close line and incinerator.

And see a dog, one end of a dirty rope tied around its neck, the other to the clothes line pole.

Chapter 42

> *"Death is part of who we are. It guides us. It shapes us . . ."*
> Christopher Paolini Brisinar

Rose rushes to the living dog and tries to lick its face. Two plastic bowls lay on their sides in the dirt, both empty. Dried up dog shit lies in the dirt.

Does the living dog feel Rose's presence? I can't tell. It lies still in the dirt, not asleep, but unmoving, most likely thirsty and hungry. Like Rose this dog is much too thin, but this dog is black, with feathery fur and dirt-caked paws. I recognize the rope—it's the same kind Rose had tied around her neck.

Can it be? Can this be where Rose suffered when she was alive? And is this poor creature her replacement?

I think about how hot it must have been out here today—it's not unusual for September days in LA to be in the 100's—then turn back toward the house, its windows now filled with a soft golden light, and want to fucking kill that Nilsson guy.

Rose looks at me, her eyes imploring.

I return my gaze to the dog.

Summoning all my will, gathering up my anger and my strength—I fly to the dog and with my gray dead fingers and try to untie the rope.

First I try to unfasten the rope from the pole, then to loosen the rope from around the poor dog's neck, but my hands don't work here.

My fingers pass right through the rope—the dog—everything—no matter how desperately hard I try to grasp it.

I am less than a shadow.

Chapter 43

"This parrot is no more. It has ceased to be. It's expired and gone to meet its maker. This is a late parrot. It's a stiff. Bereft of life, it rests in peace. If you hadn't nailed it to the perch, it would be pushing up the daisies. It's rung down the curtain and joined the choir invisible. This is an ex-parrot."
Graham Chapman, "Monty Python's Flying Circus"

I can't untie the fucking rope.

I cannot bring the dog food or give it water.

I can't lift the dog, carry it to a car and get her the fuck out of this hellhole.

I don't have a car. And if I did, I couldn't drive. Couldn't hold the keys or control the gas pedal or the steering wheel. My hands, my arms, my ample body—they don't function in the living world.

Even if I had a cell phone, I can't call 911 and report the dog's feloniously abusive owner to the police. I can't yell for one of the neighbors to help. My voice is silenced here.

In life, I admit, I was pretty fucking useless, but this—this is tragic and ridiculous.

Rose tries to lick the dog again, then looks at me, expectant.

But I can do nothing, nothing at all for this thirsty, hungry, suffering dog.

Chapter 44

> *"Dead, we are revealed in our true dimensions, and they are surprisingly modest."*
> Michael Cunningham, The Hours

I float in circles while Rose hovers, head on paws, dejectedly. We are back in our cozy corner of the annihilated after-world. Rose was reluctant, but finally she left the living dog and returned with me.

I need to clear my head, to think. And this is the finest and most private place for that.

And I couldn't think straight watching that dog suffer what Rose suffered. I can't figure things out while wanting to crush that fucking sadist Nilsson's windpipe with my bare, chubby hands, while hoping to tear his big pink head right off his neck, to stick my chubby fingers in his pale blue eyes and his mother's eyes, too.

I need some distance from the living—from their suffering. I float in circles above Rose like a supernatural smoke ring or a hologramic snake biting its own ass.

What must I do?
Save the dog.
What can I do?   Nothing.
What do I know?
I will not rest until that dog is free.

Chapter 45

> *"Even in the grave, all is not lost."*
> *Edgar Allan Poe*

First law of dead physics: The dead cannot act directly upon the living.

And even if we could, our actions would be subtle and oblique. Think ghosts. Spectres. Apparitions. Spooks.

I do not kid myself that this law will ever change. Or that Rose and I will become any less dead.

Second law of dead physics: The dead do not act; they know.

Knowing is how we will, if we will at all, somehow transcend our appalling lack of physicality.

I've learned all I can about that dog. But I'm sure I'm missing something. Something big.

Chapter 46

"I do not carry a sickle or scythe. I only wear a hooded black robe when it's cold. And I don't have those skull-like facial features you seem to enjoy pinning on me from a distance. You want to know what I truly look like? I'll help you out. Find yourself a mirror while I continue."
Markus Zusak, The Book Thief

Rose and I ooze—like The Blob through a window screen—through the delicate but powerful membrane that divides our worlds—dead us—living you—into the brightly lit front office of the 24-Hour Psychic on La Brea. All I know is that it's night in your world. I've completely lost track of days.

I picked this place because it's always open, because of the large red neon sign outside, and the cheerful Christmas lights and kitschy Egyptian statues in the window—Anubis, dog god of Death; Ammit, Eater of the Dead, with his head of a crocodile, torso of a leopard and legs and fat ass of a hippo. Also because I drove past it often going to AndyCo. after a detour to Bob's Donuts or to the airport.

The decor is black and white with red walls on which hang dream catchers, crystals, ankhs, and crosses and a little sign that says, "All Credit Cards Accepted." What? No Mogen Davids? There is a white plastic sofa and a table covered with a black tablecloth, candles, a crystal globe, and a Ouija Board. Rose is tense. She's been this way since our visit to the living dog.

I don't blame her. I'm desperate, too. Why else would anyone come here?

Rose and I hover like hummingbirds, one fat and graceless, one slim and delicate, over the woman I presume to be the psychic and her client.

If the psychic feels the presence of two dead beings right above her head, she doesn't let on.

The psychic, an ample woman in late middle age, sits behind a table. She wears a white Mexican blouse and a turquoise shawl, and her black hair, threaded with silver, hangs in loose curls around her wrinkled face. Her eyebrows have been penciled into a surprised expression; red lipstick bleeds from the edges of thin lips onto her mouth. But her long fingers are delicate and rest lightly on the planchette that sits upon a wooden Ouija board.

Across from her is a woman about my age, slender, pale, with white-blonde short hair dyed hot pink at the tips, and wearing faded jeans, flip flops and a pink t-shirt. She leans toward the medium.

"He's been missing for 5 weeks. I filed a missing person's report, but nothing's happened. I need to know if he's okay," the client says. "Can you find out if he's still alive?"

"We are not alone," the psychic announces suddenly in a deep and gravelly smoker's voice, but she does not even glance up to the space Rose and I occupy right above her head. "We are not alone," she repeats melodramatically " I can feel it, I can feel the presence of the dead."

The blonde's eyes widen.

"Go ahead. Ask them what you wish."

"Where is Brian? Is Brian alive?" the woman asks, looking at the board, then at the empty white couch, as if perhaps the dead had parked themselves in the only remaining place to sit.

"One question at a time," the psychic cautions.

"Is Brian alive? I need to know. Is Brian alive?" the blonde repeats softly, staring at the board.

The planchette takes off across the board in three diagonal streaks.

"Y. E. S." reads the psychic slowly, one letter at a time. "Yes. Your Brian. He is still among the living."

Tears roll down the blond woman's cheeks. She wipes them away and grips the table.

"Oh, God. Thank you!" she cries out. "Oh. I'm so relieved."

The psychic smiles and steals a quick glance at her watch, "The dead, they have come here to help you. But they cannot leave the Other Side for very long. You may ask them one more question."

Rose doesn't react to the scene below, just hovers in place with what has become her permanently worried expression. The only Brian I knew died in a car accident the summer I graduated from high school.

The woman swallows, then looks down at the planchette on board. "Where is Brian? Where is Brian now?"

The medium closes her eyes and waits, her fingers barely touching the planchette, which trembles for a moment and then stalls.

Howdy do as Happy Andy used to say at the end of every show. The planchette has ceased its travels around the board.

Chapter 47

"The power of the dead is that we think they see us all the time. The dead have a presence. Is there a level of energy composed solely of the dead? They are also in the ground, of course, asleep and crumbling. Perhaps we are what they dream."
Don DeLillo, White Noise

That psychic is full of shit, I know. Brian the Missing is probably in Reno. But besides making me desperate, death has made me superstitious. So little happens to me now that each event overflows with portent.

I cannot let go of the matter of the Missing Brian.

Which is why Rose and I have returned to the LAPD Administration building, this time to the Detective Support and Vice Division on the 6th floor. Uniformed officers and women and men in business attire walk through the hall carrying paper cups of coffee like extras in a movie. I've noticed that the longer I am dead, the more the world of the living loses its credibility.

Rose and I float side by side to a large bulletin board outside the closed double doors of the Missing Persons Unit. One sheet announces, "MOST MISSING RETURN HOME": "Of the 3200 adult missing persons reported annually, 70% are found or voluntarily return within 48 to 72 hours. Not all adult missing persons are the victims of kidnapping, murders, or some other criminal act."

Another instructs the reader that "BEING MISSING IS NOT A CRIME":

Being a "voluntary" missing person is not a crime. Any adult person can simply walk away, and choose to ignore family, friends, associates and employers. Since this type of behavior is not "criminal," law enforcement is limited on how they conduct these types of investigations. When facts and circumstances indicate a strong possibility of "foul-play", or the disappearance is the result of a criminal act, the investigation will continue along such a course.

I marvel at the quotation marks—in "foul-play," "criminal," and "voluntary"—then wonder if Brian decided to get the fuck out of his life or "life"—no matter how concerned or nice that blond girl seemed to be.

Rose floats near a poster entitled "HERE'S WHAT YOU CAN DO," and for a brief moment I wonder if she can read. She keeps going until she reaches a locked glass case in which is a bulletin board posted with photographs.

If death has taught me anything, it's that no special powers accompany our dissolution. It is I who reads the paper:

Provide birth date or age, physical description, medical information, circumstances surrounding the disappearance and the last location where the missing person had been seen or was known to be.

Provide any known associates and telephone numbers of persons who know the missing person.

Provide cell phone numbers, email address, and social network information.

Check local area hospitals, homeless shelters, Los Angeles County Sheriff "Inmate Locator" website, Los Angeles County Coroner and the Los Angeles County Morgue.

The blonde must have done these things already, including a consultation with the "Inmate Locator." Why else would she have nothing left to do but visit a psychic in the middle of the night?

Rose stays near the display case, then paws the air. I drift to her side, looking where she looks. There are so many photographs on this board, some stapled over the edges of others, many faded with almost illegible dates on the bottom from the 1990s. I study the faces. Good looking middle-aged men; lovely young women; old men, some smiling some frowning. Bald men. Men with mullets. Women in full makeup and women whose shiny scrubbed faces reflect the flashbulb. Last seen downtown. Last seen in Encino. Last seen going to work in Northridge. Last seen dropping off children at a daycare business in Silverlake.

I don't know any of these lost people. But Rose keeps pawing, almost frantic. I look again, then notice a picture has fallen from the board and lies face up in the glass below:

Name: Bingham, Brian K.
Missing: August, 20, 2013
Age: 26
Sex: Male
Descent: Caucasian
Height: 5'11"
Weight: 162 lbs.
Hair: Dyed purple (Brn)
Eyes: Brown
Missing from: Los Angeles
Report #: 13-576638
Circumstances: Last seen around San Julian Street, L.A.

Above those words is a pixilated color photo of a young, unsmiling man. His hair is dyed bright purple and spider tattoos cover his face.

Chapter 48

"Death is nothing to us, since when we are, death has not come, and when death has come, we are not."
Epicurus

Rose and I have returned to the afterworld. The other side. The nether realm. The not so great beyond. Purgatory. Whatever the fuck place this is—we're here.

I've begun to think that death's architecture is honeycombed—with an infinite number of discrete and silent chambers, each sheltering an occupant (or two) who toils for eternity toward his own small truth—and maybe, peace.

I know that face. But at first I couldn't place it.

It takes some probing to locate the purple hair and spider tattoos in my memory. There is no voice connected to it, no vivid event or important place. And then I recall our nocturnal visit to the Wings of Hope, Rose and I oscillating slowly over the dormitory residents as they slept.

The blond girl and the police must have checked the homeless shelters already. Maybe Brian fell and hit his purple head and then forgot completely who he was? Or maybe he was robbed, attacked, and left with nothing, not even his own memories? Perhaps his is an amnesiac's existence on Skid Row?

Most likely he's just gotten the fuck out of Dodge. He's dumped the blonde and started over with someone else, divesting himself of whoever Brian was and lying low—without the need of credit cards or things that might keep the old Brian visible.

Skid Row must be a very good place for disappearing. Almost as good as this.

Rose looks at me, one ear higher than the other.

Okay. I admit it. Searching for the Missing Brian was another crap idea of mine—like the time in college I started an FM radio station called KFK—KFUK–KFOLK—get it?

I know, I say to Rose, I haven't forgotten: The one that's important is that dog.

Chapter 49

> *"By daily dying, I have come to be."*
> Theodore Roethke

I marvel at handsome Mr. Nilsson's ease, his cheerful competence. He has a folksy manner, a wide smile, a ready laugh. In life I would have envied his athletic grace, the way he makes his way among the living, happy to stop and chat with the people that he meets.

Early this morning though, while it was still dark and the sound of his neighbors' air conditioning units masked the sounds, he didn't smile as he wrenched his dog's neck until it howled, then silenced the howl with two vicious kicks.

Rose and I are following the sadistic Mr. Nilsson. We're on his worthless ass and won't let up. We occupy his shadow in the sunlight. We are twin darknesses within his night. Rose is subdued in his presence, and holds her head low, her body taut, so close to me that if we were visible, we'd look a little like Ammit—one creature with a dog's head and a big fat ass.

We trail Nilsson through the hospital like the dead skin a snake hasn't finished shedding. If he senses our ominous, vengeful presence, he doesn't let on.

Mr. Nilsson is a busy and important man. This morning he runs a meeting in a large conference room not far from his large office. His secretary—her name is Beverly—has placed a pen and a fresh pad of lined yellow paper opposite six of the seats, has set up a cardboard carton of Starbuck coffee, paper cups, stirrers, sugar and little containers of cream in the middle of the polished table. There is a paper plate holding some muffins and some protein bars.

Two men in suits enter, then a thirtyish brunette in scrubs, and two people wearing white coats over their clothes, their names embroidered on the chest pockets.

One of the men dressed in a suit wears an ID badge: "H. Michael Patterson, CMO."

I drift close and read the woman's pocket: "Dr. K. Justing, Cardiology," then the man's: "Dr. I. Miller, Emergency Medicine" on the other.

Could this be the elusive Dr. Miller? Or should I say my Dr. Miller? A witness to my transit from this world into the other?

Mr. Nilsson's voice is friendly. "Thanks for coming so early, everybody. Now that post -mortems are no longer routine, meetings like these are hard to fit into the hospital schedule."

Nilsson nods to the woman in scrubs. "We might as well begin with the E.R."

Dr. Miller has brought a file, then and opens it, then begins to read, "On 8-27-13, the patient, age 26, was admitted to the ER and presented with syncope and numbness in his legs. He reported several previous transitory episodes of loss of consciousness during the previous weeks, but at the time of admission was uncommunicative and confused about the duration and times these episodes occurred."

One of the suits, Patterson, nods.

"Patient reported dizziness, nausea and abdominal discomfort prior to the episode. A preliminary examination could not exclude cardiogenic origin for the patient's symptoms. Dr. Justing was called for a consult."

Dr. Justing nods toward Dr. Miller. Mr. Nilsson smiles.

Dr. Justing opens her file, then speaks. "Because the patient presented with confusion and weakness, and with bradycardia in the SA node, I took the step of ordering a cardiac catheterization. The patient tolerated the procedure well. Unfortunately, while in recovery the patient suffered a cerebral vascular accident that rendered him comatose. The patient expired ten days later."

"Thank you very much, Dr. Justing," Nilsson says, then turns to the second man wearing a suit.

"Mr. Carson, how do you gauge our vulnerability to lawsuit? And in the eventuality that the patient's survivors sue, how large is our exposure to liability?"

"Was the patient able to sign a release before the procedure?" Patterson asks.

This guy is almost as smooth as Nilsson. " Yes. I've reviewed the case and don't find openings for survivors who might choose to litigate." Carson looks down again at his papers, "And I've done some research that I think will be good news: The patient— Mr. Brian K. Bingham—was, for the last 11 months, a resident at a halfway house in Skid Row where he had been a participant in a drug recovery program. To date, no family members have claimed his remains. He left foster care at age 18."

Chapter 50

"One who dies lusting for life in this world or for salvation in the next is not enlightened. In the Zen tradition, to die is nothing special."
Sushila Blackman

Brian The Missing, purple-haired and spider-tattooed, is now Brian the Dead. Alas, poor Brian, who died alone like me, right here in Nilsson's hospital. Does Rose feel how weird this is or sense my agitation?

I don't know. Her whole being is fixed upon Nilsson. When he moves, she shrinks involuntarily. When he lifts a hand, she flinches.

Nilsson bares his teeth again to mimic a smile, but it's not as wide as usual.

"A sad and unfortunate case. Let's hear from pathology."

The woman in scrubs nods, "Toxicology panels revealed high levels of heroin and THC. My examination makes me believe that the patient smoked heroin 4-6 hours before he was admitted."

This news causes the man in the suit to lean forward. "Is it possible the heroin caused the stroke?"

The pathologist glances at the other physicians, then nods. "It could. But there is no way, really, to be sure what caused the CVA—the catheterization or the patient's drug use."

Chapter 51

> *"We are but dust and shadow."*
> Horace, The Odes of Horace

Slate colored clouds hang low over the narrow beach that extends below the 101 freeway, just north of the Ventura County line. The tide advances in steel gray folds that rise and collapse against the dark, wet sand. Two joggers in the distance wear sweatshirts and long pants, so it must be cool.

I wonder if Rose's paws ever touched sand, if she's ever seen the ocean. She floats behind me, keeping her feet above the wet sand and herself far from the wave foam as if to protect herself from the spray she can neither touch nor feel.

Rose and I are here for the Missing Brian's funeral, if you can call this modest send-off that. We are here to say farewell and welcome to nowhere to a man we never knew.

The blonde, barefoot with purple nail polish on her toes, wears black leggings and a pink hooded sweatshirt. She carries a white cardboard box carefully—as if it's full of eggs or baby birds. With her is a woman who must be her mother—same body type but thicker—and her hair is brown. She holds a few purple flowers, chrysanthemums, I think, but dyed an impossible purple, the kind I used to see sometimes in the supermarket, and a helium balloon printed with the words, "I Love You." The balloon bobs impatiently back and forth in the stiff breeze, as if it's eager to be free.

A middle-aged man with short black hair walks behind the blonde. He wears jeans and a windbreaker. His fast pace through the sand and his large shoulders make me think that he's a boxer.

The small group stops, and those wearing shoes remove them. The blonde hands the box to her mother, then bends down and rolls her leggings up above her knees. The blonde takes possession of the box again and walks slowly toward the sea.

She walks until the water is knee-deep. The others follow. Rose and I float above them with the balloon.

The blond girl sighs, swallows and then speaks, tears streaming down her face, smearing her thick black eyeliner and dark mascara, "I love you, Brian," she sobs. "I don't know what happened to make you violate your ten months of sobriety. You must have had a good reason to do what you did. I'll always love and trust you."

A large wave threatens her balance and she hugs the box tightly. Her mother shivers and tightens her hold the flowers and the balloon's string. The water must be terribly cold.

The bald man pats the blonde's shoulder. "During the time I knew Brian, I learned to appreciate and to respect him. He was one of the most successful and committed residents in our rehab program. His relapse will always be a mystery to me. The thing about Brian was, he cared about other people, not just himself. I know he wanted to be a tattoo artist some day. I hope he can realize his dreams now that he's in Heaven."

Tattoo artist in heaven? Good fucking luck.

The mother nods and the girl opens the box, revealing a plastic bag inside. She lifts the bag, loosens the top, waits until a wave arrives, then pours its contents—Brian's ashes—– into the roiling sea. The breeze carries some of the gray, gritty dust away, but the rest sinks quickly under the swirling gray water and hissing foam.

The blonde's body shudders with her sobs. Her mother gently hands her some of the purple flowers, then gives one to the man and keeps one for herself.

"God bless you, Brian," the mother says, throwing the flower into the hungry waves.

"Goodbye, Brian," the man with black hair says, and tosses his flower into the water.

The blonde holds her flowers for a moment, then lets them fall into the sea. She lifts the hand holding the helium balloon high, then opens her fist to release the string.

"Goodbye, Brian. Goodbye!"

The balloon zigzags upward, and then finds a current of air and rides it quickly out to sea. It's as if the blonde, her mother, the man, and Rose and I watch Brian, who's now just a small dark shape, dissolve into the troubled sky.

Chapter 52

> *"I never understood why when you died, you didn't just vanish, everything should just keep going on the way it was only you just wouldn't be there. I always thought I'd like my own tombstone to be blank. No epitaph, and no name. Well, actually, I'd like it to say 'figment'."*
> Andy Warhol

We hang like broken light fixtures below one of the beige ceilings in the Memorial Medical Center, the place Mr. Nilsson spends his waking hours—even some weekends—except for trips to the gym, to Costco, to Starbucks and his house, which he visits overnights through very early in the mornings when sometimes he feeds and waters the dog and sometimes he doesn't. Mr. Nilsson spends his life talking on the phone, reading printouts or typing numbers and then printing more long sheets of paper covered with more numbers.

He has meetings. With people from human resources, billing, and collections, janitorial, parking. He speaks often about revenues and projections. If I weren't dead already, I'd be dead of boredom. But Rose's vigilance does not lessen; her fear of Nilsson does not cease.

What have I learned?

Cruelty and pain are often hidden.

This is going to be a "great year" for "MMC"—Memorial Medical Center, A Medical Corporation—if a record number of sick and dying people can be considered "great." It's Nilsson's job to see numbers—not people. And because numbers equal dollars, Nilsson is astoundingly, relentlessly cheap.

My thorough powerlessness—to free that dog—to expose Nilsson's cruelty—to help Rose find peace—must be, I now believe, a punishment for something I did or failed to do in life.

Something bad, something really terrible, that I must fix, must pay for. But how?

Chapter 53

"I told him I believed in hell, and that certain people, like me, had to live in hell before they died, to make up for missing out on it after death, since they didn't believe in life after death, and what each person believed happened to him when he died."
Sylvia Plath, The Bell Jar

All I know about atonement is here, at the San Fernando Valley Jewish Center, a Conservative Congregation, august location of my Bar Mitzvah and my shit brother Mark's Bar Mitzvah and my cousin Sheila's wedding.

Rose and I float inside the crowded synagogue, black polyester, embroidered and crocheted kippot like little flying saucers below us on the men's heads, tallitot on their shoulders— hairspray and cashmere on the women. I didn't bother to look for my shit brother Mark and his wife Helen, among these living people—years ago he switched to a shul over the hill that is far more hip and much better for business than this one.

Rose and I have been here since last evening (your time) appearing just before sunset in time to see the ark opened, the torah removed, and to hear the hazzan sing the Kol Nidre:

Kol Nidre (All Vows)

Prohibitions, oaths, consecrations, vows that we may vow, swear, consecrate, or prohibit upon ourselves, from this Yom Kippur until the next Yom Kippur, may it come upon us for good, regarding them all, we regret them henceforth. They will all be permitted, abandoned, cancelled, null and void, without power and without standing. Our vows shall not be valid vows; our prohibitions shall not be valid prohibitions; and our oaths shall not be valid oaths.

It's Yom Kippur, the Jewish Day of Atonement, time of ritual fasting and self-examination in preparation for the new lunar year that began last week on Rosh Hashanah, when God turned a new page in the Book of Life.

After the Kol Nidre is sung, all deals are off, and last year's promises are no longer valid. Yom Kippur decides whose names will be inscribed in Life's book and whose will not.

I know, of course, that my name will not appear. And being dead, I've got the fasting covered.

It's the repentance, the expiation of my—failures? Sins?—I am seeking in this place.

I start with commandments honored and commandments broken:

I have not had strange gods before G-D. I've had, in fact, no gods at all. I do not believe in YOU. I do not believe in myself.

I did not make any graven image. Not even one.

I have often taken the Lord my G-D's name in vain. But only metaphorically.

I failed to keep the Sabbath holy.

I did not always honor my father or my mother.

Nor they, me.

On the bright side, I did not, that I'm aware of, kill. Of course I wasn't vegan, but does that count?

I did not steal except for an illegal video stream or two.

I did not commit adultery. Lately. And when I did it was not without provocation.

I didn't bear false witness against my neighbor (except those times I lied to avoid jury duty).

I did not covet my neighbor's house or fields, nor his male or female slaves, nor his ox or ass, or anything that belonged to him.

Well, maybe my neighbor's ass.

On the bima the rabbi leads the congregation in prayer, then reads the Book of Jonah from the Torah. Even Jonah, it seems was not beyond God's reach, was not too lost to find redemption.

I contemplate, once again, my many failures, my transgressions, my arrogance, my stupidity, my selfishness. It's a shitload to revisit but I do, then add to the list of major fuck ups the biggest and the most important—my failure to help Rose.

As the sun sets over the world of the living, the Rabbi recites the Yiskor, the Prayer for the Dead, then the Shema, and the hazzan blows the shofar to signal the end of the service.

Forgive me, Happy Andy, for I have sinned.

Mr. Nilsson is probably at Costco buying muffins and coffee at a discount. And his dog is still suffering on that rope.

Chapter 54

> *"In the midst of life, we are in death."*
> Agatha Christie, *And Then There Were None*

It's Celebrate Community Day at the so-called Great Park near City Hall. Portable toilets are set up at one end and food trucks are parked on the periphery. Rose and I drift past them, and I slow down, imagining the smells that must emanate from them like auras—pad thai, grilled bratwurst, hamburgers, Korean short ribs with kimchi, black beans and rice. Once a fat man, always a fat man.

Rose gives me a questioning look and, ashamed, I remember that her experience with food was tragically limited.

We sail over the hundred or so white rental chairs that have been arranged in perfectly straight rows before a raised platform on which two women test a microphone, above trash cans placed at regular intervals, shiny white plastic trash bags lining each one, and picnic tables covered in bright blue plastic tablecloths.

The industrious Mr. Nilsson, casual in jeans and a blue MMC t-shirt, pops inside the large bloodmobile parked on the grass. The outside is painted with the MMC logo and a smiling drop of blood that says, "Save a Life!"—then Nilsson hurries to a white truck where plastic flats of bottled water and plastic bottles of orange juice are being unloaded by a two young men. Nilsson points to the bloodmobile, and they nod, Nilsson is definitely hands-on. He supervises the installation of thick balloon rainbows over a canvas

"MMC WELLNESS!" banner and counts the number of t-shirt boxes piled behind the Volunteer Check In Tables.

A fire truck arrives. Then someone in a Smokey the Bear costume. Mimes. Clowns. Face-painters. People scurry about, unpacking boxes of brochures and product samples, opening umbrellas, and taping thick electrical wires to the pavement. I see that most wear t-shirts representing an organization or a business, among them: LAPD (navy blue); Alpine Fat-Free Yogurt (powder blue); LA Open Clinic (yellow); TreeFolk (dark green); Animal Rescue LA (beige); Mamacita's Tortilla Chips (brown), Fruity Juiceee (red), and—why am I surprised?—Happy Andy Snack Foods (cheese ball orange), Wings of Hope (white).

It makes perfect sense that a homeless shelter would participate in this event. And Wings of Hope is just around the corner at Skid Row. And my shit brother, Mark—is he here? I don't see him, but recognize Patrick and a few others from the warehouse—Mark never passes up a chance for free advertising or for what he likes to call "brand enhancement."

Rose's distress propels her—us—back into our tight orbit around Nilsson. Right now he holds a clipboard and laughs with one of the bloodmobile nurses, "Sarah, don't tempt me! Those white chocolate chip cookies are my downfall. Save them all for the blood donors. I think today we'll break last year's record."

Rose looks so sad, so worried, and so tired. I hate this man. I fucking hate him. His easy manner. But most of all I hate his folksy laugh. How did Hamlet's father do it? How did he free himself, night after night, from death's exile and occupy the world of air?

How can I accomplish what he did?

Maybe I'm not trying hard enough. Maybe, as I did in life, I've given up too easily and too soon.

I sail toward a uniformed policewoman who stands at a food truck where she's placing an order. I lower myself until my head is an inch or two from her face.

"I want to report a crime," I yell. "A crime in progress!" I bellow, louder now. "You must send a police car to 22282 Circle Drive, the Nilsson residence, right away! That's mid city. Carthay Circle. A dog there is being horribly abused. This dog could die!"

"No kimchi with the chicken bowl," she says. "Did you get that? My partner doesn't like kimchi, but if it's okay, I'll take his."

Hamlet's dead father only spoke to him, to his son, I remember then. Sure he appeared to others, but vaguely. No message was delivered until his son appeared.

Perhaps the way this dead-to-living communication thing works is that the deceased can only reach one person, one important person, the only one with the power to make the things happen that must happen if there is to be justice, any justice at all.

There is only one living person who can make a difference.

Frantic, I fly above the milling people to Rose, to Nilsson, then dive, my fat ass rising in the air above my head, grasping Nilsson's neck with my hands, then squeezing with all my strength.

"You asshole!" I yell.

You would think this much cold, dead hate would amount to something, wouldn't you? That injustice would make a tiny blip on the universal radar, that Rose's suffering and the living dog's pain would thin the life/death membrane just enough to allow me one brief opening? Just one?

But my great and desperate efforts—to be heard by the living and to murder Nilsson— result in nothing. Not even a small hiccup, a tiny shudder, a blink, or the clearing of the sadistic Mr. Nilsson's throat.

Chapter 55

"Rosencrantz: We might as well be dead. Do you think death could possibly be a boat?Guildenstern: No, no, no... Death is...not. Death isn't. You take my meaning. Death is the ultimate negative. Not-being. You can't not-be on a boat.Rosencrantz: I've frequently not been on boats.Guildenstern: No, no, no—what you've been is not on boats."
Tom Stoppard, Rosencrantz and Guildenstern Are Dead

This is hell.

I'm sure of that now. Not just for me, but for Rose, too. There she is by the stage, bereft and floating in her tormentor's, her murderer's shadow, looking at me as if to say, "Follow, too."

How fucked up is that? And being stuck with me for eternity—how's that for punishment? And for what? What could this innocent sweet creature have ever thought or done to deserve what she suffered in life and suffers afterwards?

I know what you're thinking. Karma. Re-in-fucking-carnation, right? Perhaps, you'd say to me—if I could fucking hear you here—"Hey, Charlie, maybe the view you're taking of your situation isn't long enough. Maybe in a past life Rose or that dog did something really bad. Maybe that dog was Hitler. And maybe Rose was Pol Pot."

Well, fuck you.

And the cloud of incense you rode in on.

You've got to be fucking kidding.

And if it's not you who's kidding, maybe it's God. Or Krishna. Or the Buddha. Or Jesus. Or Allah. Or Something that's part of the structure of the universe—maybe dark matter is composed of suffering. Maybe pain is the cosmic glue that holds the world together.

I know I've fucked things up real good. But give me another thousand lives and another thousand deaths, and I bet I'll fuck those up, too.

Why wouldn't I? I'm a piece of shit. I'm worthless.

But not Rose. And not that dog, whose time is running out. They mean something. They are valuable. They are good.

The fault must lie in me, not in the fucking stars. I get it, now—this hell is me.

Fine. I accept the terms and conditions of my eternal nonexistence.

But there's one last thing I have to do and have to say to Whoever or Whatever is In Charge—Enough.

I sincerely pray, beg, request, ask and humbly implore of Thee, leave Rose and the dog out of this.

Let their suffering be mine, all mine.

Chapter 56

"The wages of sin are death, but by the time taxes are taken out, it's just sort of a tired feeling."
Paula Poundstone

The park grounds are crowded with people now, many of them children who climb aboard the fire truck or take free samples from the various tables and displays. Two men with dreadlocks are on the stage, playing electric guitars and singing "Good Morning, Sunshine."

For a moment I can't locate Rose, but then I see her, to the left of the stage, hovering above Nilsson who is chatting with a man. I float to Rose, and though she can't feel it here, I gently stroke her worried forehead.

How do I tell her that I've failed her? How do I explain that it's time to leave?

That we must abandon the living permanently?

That I can do nothing to save the dog?

Now I am right above the man talking with Nilsson. The muscles of the man's tanned arms and of his large shoulders are sharply defined, even under the white t-shirt he's wearing. His hair is black, and short.

"I heard last delivery had a problem," the man says.

A girl in pigtails pushes between the two men and Nilsson smiles at her and she smiles back.

"That can't happen again," the man says after she's out of earshot.

The music is louder now. People are clapping and singing along. I move in, almost beneath Rose's belly, and can see WINGS OF HOPE printed on the front of his t-shirt. Then I look at his face.

This is the same guy we saw at Brian's funeral at the beach.

The guy who looks like a boxer.

"Don't worry," Nilsson says, unsmiling now and almost grim, "It won't. That's all taken care of. And I'll make damn sure nothing like that happens again."

Chapter 57

"Death is as unexpected in his caprice as a courtesan in her disdain; but death is truer – Death has never forsaken any man."
Honoré de Balzac

I try to pry Rose loose from Nilsson. She's with him as he joins a group of "community leaders"—representatives from TreeFolk, Community Clinic, and Alpine Yogurt—onstage with the Mayor, the Chief of Police and a few members of the City Council, as cameras flash.

She shadows him right inside the Bloodmobile, then flits over his head like a butterfly while he pretends to donate blood and a professional photographer from the L.A. Times takes pictures of him smiling, then drinking a cup of orange juice and eating a chocolate cookie.

Rose stays close, circling him as he smiles—Nilsson is a champion smiler—next to him as he schmoozes one person and then another, or helps a group of volunteers sign in at the MMC tables.

"Rose," I call out almost sharply, "Rose." I've never spoken to her this way before in death or during our visits to the living world. I've always addressed her gently and as my equal—one dead being to another.

Rose stays close to Nilsson but she looks at me, surprised.

Then I speak to her as I've heard living people speak to their living dogs, giving her not a command, exactly, but making a sternly expressing an expectation: "Rose, come. Come with me. Now."

Rose watches as Nilsson smilingly receives a tall Starbucks coffee from a woman in a blue MMC t-shirt, then returns her gaze to me once, her brown eyes large and doubtful.

"Come, Rose. Come. Come with me now. Come on, Rosie, please."

Chapter 58

> *"Alive. Alive in the way that death is alive."*
> John Fowles, The Collector

The dying mid-September afternoon streaks the yellow sky with clouds. The jangly sounds of steel drums from the Celebrate Community event in the Great Park reach the people here on San Julian Street. We float opposite a regal middle-aged man in stained tuxedo pants, a red sweatshirt and flip flops with mismatched socks—one white, one green— as he guards an overflowing shopping cart outside the entrance to Wings of Hope. He must be waiting for the evening meal, I think.

"Oh Lord!, Oh, Jesus! Bless you this street. Oh God, bless this sidewalk!" The man has dropped to his knees, and deep-voiced, shouts his exhortations at the dirty sidewalk. Then he swivels his head to survey the people near him. "Oh, Heavenly God, bless that man with the blue blanket! Lord, shower the woman with that cigarette with your love!"

The man with the blanket and the woman with the cigarette receive these intercessions with aplomb, as if they've heard all this before, though one guy, a lean and handsome African American man with an Afro that sits like a halo on his head, nods and says, "Amen, brother. Amen."

Tuxedo man springs to his feet, surprisingly agile, and withdraws an empty wine bottle from his cart, then waves it around for emphasis. I wished I could meet Christopher Smart. Well, here, in a way, he is.

"This bottle is holy! This cart is holy!" he declares. "This trash bag is holy!" He waves a tattered black bag for all to contemplate, then drops it into the cart. "This, this bathrobe right here, right now is holy!" He extracts a woman's pink and yellow chenille bathrobe from the cart. The sleeves and hem are singed, as though it had been rescued from a fire. And full of holes.

"God bless this!" he shouts, agitated now, lifting an empty potato chip bag from the curb. "God bless nothing!" he screams, focusing his intent, wild eyes exactly on the space Rose and I invisibly occupy, then sending the wine bottle through my forehead and onto the littered street where it explodes.

Rose trembles, fear shuddering through her in waves. I pull her close to me.

As the bottle travels through me, I flinch, but Rose cowers, shrinking into herself, reflexively afraid of being hurt, expecting the pain that she received in life. I am so sorry to bring Rose here, but I must find the muscular black-haired guy we saw with Nilsson—the same man, I'm sure, now, who attended the Missing Brian's melancholy funeral.

I scratch the soft fur behind Rose's ears, massage her neck, but she's still nervous. This guy—the one who looks like a boxer—he does some kind of work at Wings of Hope.

Chapter 59

> *"Please don't die."*
> Randy Pausch, The Last Lecture

Supper is served late at Wings of Hope because of the disturbance. A black and white, siren howling, arrived soon after the bottle shattered. Two male uniformed officers, both wearing latex gloves, emerged, and examined the broken bottle as if it might be radioactive or explosive. After that they conversed quietly with Tuxedo Pants, who smiled and nodded when they pointed to the broken glass. Tuxedo Pants barely had time to bless both officers and to declare their police car holy before they threw him on the ground, forced his hands into steel cuffs, and dragged him, his flip flops falling off and breaking, his precious cart abandoned on the sidewalk, into their police car.

Dinner is somber. Rose and I hover in a corner of the large kitchen area. She's curled up, nose to tail, a few inches from the floor. I float next to her. A middle aged woman wearing a silver crucifix greets each diner by name—the man with the blanket, John; the cigarette woman, Angela; the man with the Afro, Peace—and others, some of whom are people Rose and I saw in the dorms—and some who are new to us. The woman, her name is Wendy, joins the others as they eat spaghetti and meatballs, rolls and margarine, milk or water, and canned peaches off paper plates. Two women from the night we first saw Brian— the very fat woman and the woman with corn rows—wear white aprons and white paper caps and serve the meal.

Once the meal is over, the oilcloth-covered tables are pushed against one wall, and the chairs are arranged to form a loose circle. Wendy and the others sit down, while Peace and another man sweep the floor and take out trash.

"Welcome once again to Wings of Hope," Wendy says and smiles. "God is love. All are welcome." Her short brown hair is flecked with gray and the constellation of freckles extending across her nose and cheeks stands out because she wears no makeup. I guess she's in her forties. "Thank you for being here and for participating once again in our Support Circle."

Wendy's smile seems genuine. She smiles with her eyes, her mouth, her face—her voice—her whole body. She bestows it upon each person in the circle, even the sleeping man who snores loudly and a woman who is busy tying a plastic trash bag into a pattern of knots, then looks toward Peace and nods to him.

In life did I ever receive such a warm and sincere welcome? Was anyone ever this truly glad to see me? No. The closest I've come to anything like this was my reunion with Rose.

"Would anyone like to speak? Or should we just go around the circle like always?" Wendy asks.

Peace sits down with the group. "I have something to say." Peace shakes his head and his Afro bobs slightly in the direction opposite to the movement of his head. "I'm bummed. I'm angry." Peace surveys the circle. "And when I feel this way, sometimes bad shit happens."

Wendy looks directly at Peace. Her face is calm, full of sympathy and understanding. "I know we all feel the loss of Brian terribly," Wendy says sadly. "He was an important and beloved part of the Wings of Hope community."

"Yeah," Peace says. "What the fuck happened? One minute Brian is here and then all of a sudden he's dead." But before Wendy can answer, Peace goes on, becoming more upset. "And what about just now, huh? I'm sick of this police bullshit. Bernard was just minding his own business.

Waiting for his dinner. So what if he likes to pray? Who does that hurt? Can anybody tell me? Who does that hurt?"

Tuxedo Man has a name—Bernard.

Wendy looks sad. "What happened with Mr. Carter—Bernard—was very unfortunate. Mr. Sims is at the station now trying to see what can be done for him. But Bernard, as I understand it, threw a glass bottle at someone and that's not okay. Not okay at all. When Bernard did that, he broke the law."

Cigarette Woman speaks softly and I see that she is missing her bottom teeth, "He threw the bottle in the street. Not at anybody. Just at the street."

Peace nods emphatically. "You saying he's going to jail for littering? Or for throwing something in the street?"

Wendy sighs, but musters another smile. "I know it seems unfair. But it's important to recognize that Bernard, even if he was just blowing off steam, did that in a destructive and illegal way. That's why we're here in our community. To support one another and to find constructive ways to express feelings, and to free ourselves of violence and from addictions."

Wendy looks at Peace and waits.

He nods his understanding but his expression darkens. His jaw clenches and unclenches, he crosses his arms across his chest, and he begins to tap his foot against the linoleum floor.

Wendy continues, her voice and expression full of concern and sadness. "About Brian. It's really important that everyone understands what happened. Brian was not feeling well and at the hospital they had to perform a test to make sure that his heart was working properly. Unfortunately there were complications after that test—and Brian died. It's a tragedy, but it's no one's fault. We all must die and it was Brian's time."

Chapter 60

"That which is so universal as death must be a benefit."
Johann Friedrich Von Schiller

Wendy's a fucking saint. So kind, so generous, so selfless and so patient.

Almost as kind and as patient as Rose.

I regret not knowing Wendy in life. I mourn the lack of courage and imagination that kept me far away San Julian Street. I could have helped Wendy or someone like her help these people. Not just my Happy Andy money—me. And helping them might have changed me, might have saved me from myself.

But even Wendy cannot soothe Peace's growing and obvious agitation. She gets up from her chair and stands before him, then looks pleadingly into his angry eyes.

"Peace," she asks quietly. "Will you lead the group in a prayer for Brian?

Peace hugs himself more tightly, and taps his foot more loudly, which Wendy and I both take to be a no.

"That's okay," Wendy says, and stands. "Let's join together in a moment of silent prayer for our friend Brian's soul."

Those among the assembled who are awake lower their heads, except for the woman knotting plastic bags. Some close their eyes. Peace unfolds his arms and stands up so abruptly that he knocks over his white plastic chair. "Bullshit," he shouts, "Bullshit!" then he rushes angrily from the room.

Wendy doesn't lift her head or open her eyes—her face remains serene, her lips continue to speak their silent words of prayer for Brian. But the others, their eyes open now, listen to the click of Peace's footsteps in the hall, then to the sound of the door to San Julian Street being opened.

Chapter 61

"All say, 'How hard it is that we have to die'—a strange complaint to come from the mouths of people who have had to live."
Mark Twain, The Tragedy of Pudd'nhead Wilson and the Comedy of the Extraordinary Twins

Rose and I follow Peace outside. It's dark now and there are inert human shapes on the sidewalk, some in sleeping bags, some with only torn pieces of cardboard between them and the ground. Peace walks quickly past these forms, past the spot in the street where Bernard's broken wine bottle glitters under the street lamp—the lamp, its light reflected in the glass and the burning orange tips of cigarettes in shadowy doorways—are the only bright things.

Peace turns the corner and turns into the alley, illuminated by a few security lights installed at the back of the brick buildings. Rose and I turn with him and see a man urinate against a wall, then hurry away. Peace walks purposely to the Dumpster behind Wings of Hope. Peace opens the metal lid and rummages inside, then shuts it, and moves a few doors down. He opens a trash can and feels around inside until he's found something—two half-smoked cigarettes.

He lights one of them with a matchbook from his pocket, then carefully puts the other behind his ear where it disappears inside his Afro. Peace paces back and forth, inhaling the cigarette smoke deeply.

Rose stiffens as a dark figure appears at the opening of the alley—the shape of a man with large shoulders backlit by the light in the street.

"Peace," the dark shape says, "Is that you?"

125

Peace inhales, holding the smoke inside his lungs for a moment before answering and exhaling. "Who is it?"

The dark shape approaches. "It's me, Peace. Mr. Sims."

Peace keeps smoking, but he's stopped pacing and faces the shape. The greenish security light behind Wings of Hope reveals the same white t-shirt we saw when this man spoke with Nilsson, but the shirt is partially covered now by a leather jacket.

So this is Mr. Sims.

Sims pats Peace's shoulder. "I'm here because Wendy was worried about you. The community is worried about you. And I'm here because I'm your friend."

Peace nods. "Yeah. I know."

"Wendy says you're angry about Bernard's arrest," Sims says, "and Brian." Sims reaches into his pocket and produces two unopened packs of Marlboro cigarettes, which he gives to Peace.

"I understand. Wendy understands. But you—" and here Sims puts great emphasis on "you"—"must understand that you can't risk your sobriety every time you get upset."

Peace shakes his head, defeated. The tears that begin to roll down his smooth, dark cheeks seem greenish in this light.

"Bernard will be okay. He's only being held for 72 hours on a 51-50. For observation. Not in jail but in the psych ward at County. He'll be fine."

Peace nods again, more vigorously. His beautiful hair nods too, and in the strange light looks like a frothy aura. Finally Peace says, "I just can't take the bullshit, you know? I just can't take it."

"I understand," Sims says kindly. "I get it." Sims takes a slender leather wallet from the pocket of his leather jacket, counts out some bills, folds them in half, and presses them into Peace's hand. "You need a little break. You really need a break from this place, Peace."

Peace stuffs the bills into his pocket. "I got nothing, Mr. Sims. How can I ever pay you back? " Peace asks in a shaky voice.

"Don't worry about that, "Sims says, "we'll work it out. We'll work something out."

Chapter 62

"Life was not a valuable gift, but death was. Life was a fever-dream made up of joys embittered by sorrows, pleasure poisoned by pain; a dream that was a nightmare-confusion of spasmodic and fleeting delights, ecstasies, exultations, happinesses, interspersed with long-drawn miseries, griefs, perils, horrors, disappointments, defeats, humiliations, and despairs"—the heaviest curse devisable by divine ingenuity; but death was sweet, death was gentle, death was kind; death healed the bruised spirit and the broken heart, and gave them rest and forgetfulness; death was man's best friend; when man could endure life no longer, death came and set him free."
Mark Twain, Letters from the Earth

The world of the living is weird. Not just strange, but weird in the Anglo Saxon sense—'wyrd.'

'That which comes.' Fate. What is. Reality. Or as Wallace Stevens said in his poem, The Man on the Dump, 'the the.'

In expressed another way, shit happens. Constantly. And keeps happening. Confusing. Intractable.

And death? Don't ask. Death is another story altogether—you'll see.

Rose has assumed her patient, watchful pose—seated, paws extended, chin on paws, watching me think, and waiting, waiting, always waiting for me to free that dog. If she could breathe, she'd sigh. Too bad there's no dead squirrel here for her to chase up a big, dead tree, to distract her gaze—just for a little while—from me.

Rose, I know it doesn't look like much, but I'm trying, I'm trying to figure things out.

What I know:

Peace disappeared into the night, or more precisely, checked into a residential hotel after a visit to a liquor store and a brief transaction with a gentleman standing on a street corner.

That little scene in the alley with Peace and Sims was really sad. Sad and weird.

Weird that Sims knew Brian and Sims knows Peace and Nilsson.

Nilsson. It's weird that he knows Sims, but MMC must be a big donor to Wings of Hope.

What did Sims mean when he spoke to Nilsson about a "delivery"? Probably MMC brochures for clients of Wings of Hope. No. County Hospital is the closest medical facility to Skid Row. MMC is over in West Hollywood. And the delivery was to the hospital, not from the hospital.

Maybe it was Wings of Hope brochures for MMC? Maybe for a board meeting? Perhaps Sims is going to address the big shots there and make a pitch for money?

No. Didn't he say there was a "problem" with the delivery?

What kind of delivery, then? And what went wrong?

I need to know more about Sims.

Chapter 63

"And even if the wars didn't keep coming like glaciers, there would still be plain old death."
Kurt Vonnegut, Slaughterhouse-Five

Has one night passed in the world of the living? Or two or three? Rose and I follow slowly above Peace as he makes his way unsteadily along San Julian Street, sometimes stopping to lean on a wall for balance, ignoring the greetings of acquaintances who mill about or huddle on the curb under tarps and blankets. The heat wave is over, but Peace wears the clothes he wore when we saw him with Sims in the alley—dark jeans, black boots, a long-sleeved black t-shirt that says with a picture of Bob Marley on the back. He slept in those clothes, I think, then correct myself.

Of course he slept in those clothes. This is Skid Row.

The shadows Rose and I circulate among tell me it must be close to noon when Peace arrives at Wings of Hope entrance. We follow him down the hall, where Wendy and the fat woman sort through boxes of donated clothing. The woman who knots plastic bags is here too, sitting in a white plastic chair, tying an elaborate knot in a yellow bag.

"Peace," Wendy says and smiles. "You're back. Welcome."

Peace is subdued. The whites of his eyes are red and the lids are heavy and puffy. "Yeah. I'm back. Mr. Sims? Is he around?" he asks. His voice is raspy.

"Upstairs," Wendy says, "showing a new client around the men's dorm. I'm sure he'll be happy to see you."

Peace nods and makes his way up the stairs so slowly that I begin to wonder if he's hurt, but his pace quickens as he enters the men's dormitory.

Mr. Sims talks to a young man who looks about eighteen. The man holds a filthy white laundry bag that appears stuffed with clothes. The young man's greasy brown hair is pulled back into a ponytail. He wears tattered jeans and a jean jacket—but there is no shirt underneath. "And these are the lockers," Sims says. "When clients have checked in and completed our intake process—just like you, Manuel—they are given a key for the night for one of these lockers. The number on the key matches the locker—that way the client has a safe place to store belongings."

The young man nods, but looks bewildered.

"But there are strict rules. No smoking. No drugs. Illegal or prescription. No alcohol."

"Si," Manuel says.

Sims smiles. "There's a shower in the men's lavatory. If you need a change of clothes, we have boxes sorted by size. And there's soap, toothbrushes, toothpaste—toiletries."

"Gracias," the young man says.

Sims sees Peace leaning in the doorway and nods in his direction. "Manuel, I need to take care of something right now, okay? Here's your locker key."

Sims hands Manuel a key attached to a bright green coiled plastic keychain, the kind people wear around their wrists. "Get your things stowed and then go downstairs to Wendy. She'll help you with clothes, and you can figure out which support group will be right for you."

Manuel lets the heavy laundry bag drop to the floor, and accepts the key gratefully. Sims pats him on the back, then turns to Peace and smiles. "Peace. You look like a man who could really use a cup of coffee,"

Chapter 64

"Who knows but life be that which men call death, and death what men call life?
Euripides, Phrixus

Sims and Peace are just a few blocks away from San Julian Street, but it's a different world. The human beings in this world walk purposefully or sit, not on the ground, but in chairs or on benches.

And there are trees under the dark sky full of gathering clouds.

Rose likes this place, especially the fountain—maybe because she was so often thirsty in life. She floats behind Sims, Peace, and me close to the water, as if proximity will somehow communicate to her the sensation of its liquid coolness.

Attractive men and women in crisp shirts, pressed wool suits and silk, matched socks inside their polished shoes, eat elegant lunches outdoors at Pinot Cafe on the Central Library's patio. Salads with poached eggs and ground pepper on top; small filets mignon and grilled asparagus; espresso served in pure white demitasses. Sims and Peace sit on the edge of the long, rectangular fountain. Peace drinks from a tall paper cup of coffee.

A sandwich, still wrapped in cellophane, rests on a napkin next to him.

"Thanks, Mr. Sims," Peace says, squinting a little as if he has a headache.

"The coffee will help," Sims says, then observes a group of elementary school students ascending the shallow stone staircase into the library's main lobby, one gray haired woman leading them, a younger woman shooing them in from the rear.

"We can explore the fountain later," the young woman says to a little boy who has stopped for a moment near Sims and Peace.

Peace puts the cup of coffee on the stone ledge, unwraps the sandwich, and takes a bite. "This is good, too. Really good."

"I'm glad," Sims says. "You may not realize it, Peace, but you're important to me."

Peace looks quizzically at Sims while he chews, then says, "Me? No way, Mr. Sims. I'm not important. I'm a nobody."

Sims smiles. "Peace. You're an intelligent man and a thoughtful man. I've been looking for someone just like you to become my assistant for a special project. It's a salaried position. You'd be off the street for good."

Peace stops eating and his eyes widen. "Me? Work for you?"

Sims nods.

"That would be a dream come true, Mr. Sims. A dream come true." "But first you need to get your head together, Peace. And to do that, I think you need a real rest."

Peace nods, then smiles ruefully. "I'm tired. I'm so tired, Mr. Sims. I wish I could just sleep for days and days."

Rose has dropped to the water's surface now, hovering dreamily over the shallow pool.

Sims leans close to Peace. "I know a way. But you have to do exactly—exactly as I tell you." Sims searches Peace's face for affirmation.

"I'm listening," Peace says, interested. "It's not like I have a lot of other offers," he jokes, but Sims is serious now.

"And what I tell you is just between us, okay? Just you and me. Not even Wendy. Not Bernard. No one else can know. Understood?"

Peace nods his head. "Later today you will tell Wendy that you aren't feeling well. You'll say you have pain in the middle of your chest." Sims taps his sternum with his big hand flat and open. "You'll tell her you feel really bad. That your left arm and the left side of your jaw are hurting, too."

Peace listens intently and pauses as if to absorb what Sims has told him. Then he says, "Don't feel good. Chest hurts. Arm hurts. Jaw hurts."

"Left," Sims says almost sharply. "You have to say your left arm. Your left jaw."

"I'm sorry," Peace says. "Left. Left. I got it. " His coffee is getting cold. A gray and rust colored pigeon approaches his sandwich and starts pecking at the cellophane.

"After you tell Wendy these things, she will come to me and I will call for an ambulance that will take you to the hospital—Wings of Hope already has your Social Security Number from the Veterans' Administration."

"Hospital?" Peace says, shocked, unhappy. "Where Bernard is? I hate that hospital. I don't ever want to go there. Never."

"No," Sims explains. "Not where Bernard is. Not County. This is a different hospital, across town. You'll be fine, you'll get the rest you need. I promise. And for your trouble I'll throw in a hundred bucks."

Peace frowns while he thinks this over, and only when his expression relaxes does Sims continue. "You'll go to the emergency room and tell the nurses and doctors exactly, exactly what you told Wendy—"

"I feel bad. My chest hurts. My arm hurts. Left arm. My left jaw hurts" Peace says.

"Right!" Sims says and laughs, "I mean left. Left. And then you'll have a test."

"Test? What test?" Peace looks worried.

"It's nothing. It's routine, and perfectly safe—just a way doctors check out your heart."

"Tests are bullshit," Peace says, upset.

"Trust me," Sims says. "I always look out for you, don't I?"

"Yes," Peace says.

"And I have a good friend who works at that hospital," Sims explains. "So nothing can happen to you while he's there, absolutely nothing."

Peace watches the pigeon peck at the French roll on his sandwich, then looks at Sims and nods his assent.

Sims smiles warmly, "Just think of it as a little vacation.

You'll get to spend a few days in a nice clean bed with all the food, free TV and movies you want, while pretty young nurses wait on you hand and foot."

Chapter 65

*"If I was dead, I wouldn't know I was dead. That's the only thing I
have against death. I want to enjoy my death."*
Samuel Beckett, Eleutheria

The sky has darkened like a bruise and a few raindrops fall on San Julian Street. Despite the weather, a small crowd of people, some in black trash bag ponchos, others holding pieces of cardboard over their heads, watch as two paramedics in dark blue uniforms load Peace, covered from neck to foot in a white sheet and strapped to a gurney, into an ambulance. A worried-looking Wendy pats Peace's foot as the gurney slides inside, then stands back as the EMTs close the door. Sims is there, too, and puts his arm around Wendy's shoulder.

Rose and I enter the ambulance through the closed back door as it pulls away. Inside the narrow space crowded with equipment, one of the EMTs secures the gurney, then leans in close to Peace.

"We're taking you to the hospital to be evaluated for your chest pain," he says. "But I need to ask you some questions."

Peace nods. He looks scared, scared enough to be truly sick. Rose floats over his chest and I float next to him. The other EMT is in the front driving the ambulance. I can see through a window to the windshield wipers sweeping back and forth. The rain falls harder now. I think of the dog tied up out there, wet and cold, and if I weren't dead, would feel sick too. I fight the urge to visit the dog—I can do nothing there, I know.

"How would you describe your pain right now?"

"Bad," Peace says. "Real bad. On the left." Peace lifts his hand with it taps his sternum carefully.

The EMT nods and writes something down on a paper attached to a clipboard.

"Do you remember what you were doing and how long ago the pain started?"

Peace is silent for a moment then says, "Taking a shower. Washing my hair. Hour. Two hours ago."

The EMT notes this and continues. "What does it feel like right now? Is it sharp or dull? Is it radiating?"

"I'm not sure," Peace says after a moment.

This doesn't appear to bother the EMT, who nods. "Is it steady or does it come and go?"

"Steady."

"Do you have any allergies to medication?"

Peace shakes his head, no, then places his right hand over his sternum and leaves it there. He closes his eyes.

The EMT smiles. "Hold on, Mr. Peace. Driving in the rain in LA is crazy. But we're almost there."

Chapter 66

"You only live twice. Once when you are born and once when you look death in the face."
Ian Fleming, You Only Live Twice

Rose and I follow the EMTs as they wheel Peace through the wide swinging doors into the Memorial Medical Center ER. We observe the nurses admit him, then watch as the ER doctor—not Miller this time or that young woman, Branford—another one, an Asian man—examine Peace and order blood tests.

Peace mostly keeps his eyes closed—sleeping or pretending to sleep—despite the sounds of voices and noises in the hallway. After an hour or so the doctor returns.

"How are you doing, sir?" He asks.

Peace opens his eyes and puts his hand on his chest once again. "The pain is right here," he says. "On the left."

"Is it worse?"

"It's bad," Peace says.

"Is there a history of cardiac disease in your family?"

"No family." Peace says flatly.

"When was the last time you ate or drank anything?" the doctor asks.

"Yesterday," Peace tells him. I remember the sandwich that he left outside the library. Does one bite count as a meal? Peace remembers this too, because he changes his mind and says, "Or maybe the day before."

"Okay," the doctor says and smiles. "We're going to admit you. You'll spend the night upstairs on the cardiac floor, and then tomorrow morning, another doctor, a heart doctor named Dr. Justing, is going to run some tests."

Chapter 67

> *"The grave itself is but a covered bridge,*
> *Leading from light to light, through a brief darkness!"*
> Henry Wadsworth Longfellow, The Golden Legend

Rose has given up on me.

Her intelligent dead eyes avoid mine. When I scratch her back or stroke her head, she turns away.

I don't blame Rose. I can't stand myself, either. Bad things keep happening and I do nothing, less than nothing, to stop them.

The dog still suffers. Nilsson still roams the living world happy and free.

And then there's Peace. Scared shitless, lying in that hospital alone. I'm sure now that what happened to Missing Brian had something to do with Sims, is part of the same scam, which I can't figure out now except to know it that benefits Sims, not Peace.

I think the hospital is where everything intersects:

My death.

Rose.

Nilsson.

The dog.

Wings of Hope.

Brian's death.

Sims.

And Peace.

So, with Rose or without her, I'm going back there and figure it out.

Chapter 68

> *"Death's gang is bigger and tougher than anyone else's. Always has been and always will be. Death's the man."*
> Michael Marshall, The Upright Man

Can the dead faint?

I float alone in the Cath Lab above two nurses in scrubs and paper caps. They've already strapped Peace into a strange, thick hospital bed, and received his shaky signature on the consent form.

A paper shower cap covers most of Peace's Afro, but some hair escapes at the nape of his neck. The male nurse adjusts the cap, then pulls back the sheets and lifts the pale blue hospital gown to expose Peace's thin, muscular legs. The nurse removes a plastic razor from its package, then shaves Peace's groin. The other nurse starts an IV in Peace's arm.

Some fucking vacation. Peace looks exhausted and frightened.

"Still raining?" the male nurse asks Peace just to make conversation. Peace says nothing. What a fucking stupid question, I think, and wonder if his hospital room had a window and if it did, what Peace could see. Well I hope the view was good, full of sky and birds and trees.

"Mr. Peace," the male nurse says, "I'm going to numb your groin area now, then insert a tiny catheter. You're going to feel a pinch."

Peace flinches.

"You're doing great," the female nurse says, "In a little while the cardiologist, Dr. Justing, will insert some dye into the catheter and watch your heart in action."

Peace doesn't seem to appreciate this information and squeezes his eyes shut once more.

Dr. Justing enters in scrubs, wearing the same kind of blue hat Peace wears, and leans over Peace. "Good morning, Mr. Peace," she says. "I'm your cardiologist, Dr. Justing. I'm going to perform a procedure called an angioplasty. I'm going to put a tiny catheter into your heart, fill it with dye. A radiologist in another room with watch as the dye shows up on an x-ray. Then we'll be able to see what caused the chest pain you had yesterday."

Dr. Justing points to a large square device that extends over the bed. "This is a camera. After we inject the dye, we're going to move it around so we get a good picture of your heart. We may ask you to move, or we may move the bed. Just relax and lie still unless we tell you not to."

Peace is somber as the female nurse hands Dr. Justing a syringe. Dr. Justing injects its contents into the catheter in Peace's groin.

"You're doing great!" the nurse says again. "Just lie still."

Peace moans a little, then shouts, "I'm hot. I'm burning up!"

"That's normal," Dr. Justing says. "Don't worry. Sometimes the dye makes people feel warm. It's nothing to worry about."

Peace is quiet then starts to squirm. "I feel sick!"

His face is turning gray, and his eyes wide open in distress. "My throat! I can't breathe!"

Peace gasps, then wheezes.

"He's reacting to the contrast," Dr. Justing shouts. "Call a code! "Give him Epi 1 to 10,000. 0.1 CC."

Fuck! Fuck!

Is Peace dying? Suffocating right in front of me?

Without thinking I call out, "Rose! Rose!" then marvel at my stupidity. Who the fuck do I think Rose is? Lassie? And if she were here, what could she do?

"No BP!" shouts the male nurse, just as Rose appears beside me—yes, just like a ghost. Now both of us float together over Peace, Dr. Justing and the nurses around his bed.

"Open up the IV line. Run the IV fluids wide open! And elevate his legs!"

The other nurse produces another a bag of liquid from a cart and connects to the IV line in Peace's arm. The male nurse tips the table up so Peace's is lower than his feet.

More nurses have entered the cath lab now, with carts and equipment.

"Start 100% oxygen," Dr. Justing orders, "and a Proventil mask."

A nurse straps a mask onto Peace's gray face and attaches it to a nebulizer.

"Tachycardia of 140!" the male nurse says.

"He's in shock!" someone says. "I can't get a pressure!"

Rose drops close to Peace.

I think he's unconscious now. I can't tell if he's breathing or not behind the mask.

A monitor next to the bed begins to emit a long beeping sound.

Chapter 69

"Death is a natural part of life. Rejoice for those around you who transform into the Force."
Yoda, Star Wars Episode III

"Peace!" I yell. "Peace!" I hover close to him as he lies naked on the bed, tubes in his arm and his groin, a mask on his face. Rose drops to his chest and licks his cheek, his forehead, then emits three loud, sharp barks.

"Peace!" I yell again. "Breathe!"

Rose keeps barking, frantic now, and paws his chest.

Then the room becomes terribly quiet, as if the living earth itself took in a sharp intake of breath.

Peace opens his eyes, but Dr. Justing and the nurses don't seem to notice.

Is he breathing? I can't tell.

But he must be. He must be alive.

With his free hand, Peace pushes the nebulizer mask from his face, sits up and scans the room, then, as his wide-eyed gaze settles on something above his bed, he screams.

Chapter 70

> *"Death —the last sleep? No, it is the final awakening."*
> Sir Walter Scott

"You!" Peace screams, "and that dog. What the fuck are you?"

Whom is Peace addressing? Is it possible someone brought a service dog in here? And why are the others so fucking quiet?

"Get that dog away from me!" Peace yells again, and cowers.

Rose and I float above Peace like Macy's Thanksgiving parade balloons. We wait for the doctor and nurses to calm the patient they have just so miraculously revived. Now Rose's tail wags and she paws the air.

"Back off!" Peace yells again. His voice is hostile. Maybe after some tranquilizers he'll be himself again, I think. Jesus, after what he's just been through, it makes sense that he's disoriented.

"Fat man!" Peace screams wildly and looks right up at me. "I mean you!"

Chapter 71

"We sometimes congratulate ourselves at the moment of waking from a troubled dream: it may be so the moment after death."
Nathaniel Hawthorne, American Note-Books

Rose descends over Peace's hospital bed, but he shrinks away, crazy now and hissing, "No fucking dogs! No fucking dogs!"

I lower myself slowly, too, confused.

What did he mean when he said "fat man"?

Wait.

Peace can see Rose.

Peace sees me.

Which can only mean one thing:

Peace is dead.

Chapter 72

"Dying is a troublesome business: there is pain to be suffered, and it wrings one's heart; but death is a splendid thing —a warfare accomplished, a beginning all over again, a triumph. You can always see that in their faces."
George Bernard Shaw

We're still in the Cath lab, but Peace has left his bed.

And now there are two men who look just like him, one motionless in the bed, surrounded by frantic hospital staff, and this one, standing naked except for the paper cap. There's an orange swath of Betadine on his groin, and some blood at the catheter site. An IV tube and still hangs from his forearm.

I move back and nudge Rose back, too.

Give the poor man some space, I think then, and search my muscle-memory for an inoffensive smile. Suddenly I feel embarrassed about my weight, my bare feet and bloodstained shirt, the hole in my neck—and about being dead.

"Peace," I say calmly and try to smile, "I'm Charlie. And this," I pat Rose on the head, "This is Rose. She won't hurt you. I promise. She's a good dog. A really sweet dog." Rose wags her tail as if to demonstrate to Peace how sweet she really is.

"What's happening?" Peace asks.

Good fucking question. I wish I knew.

"I'm not exactly sure," I say, "And I'm sorry to be the one to tell you this, but I'm ninety-nine percent sure you're dead."

"I'm dead?" Peace is incredulous. He stares at me, at Rose and down at his own naked body with suspicion.

"We're dead, too. The dog and I," I say. "It's not too bad," I lie. What an ass I am. What a stupid fucking thing to say.

"Shit. What happened?" Peace looks frightened again and turns toward the nurse bending over his other body on the bed. "Nurse! Nurse!" he yells, "Help me!"

The nurse, of course, does not react at all. Peace tries to grab her shoulder but his hand dissolves.

"Something went wrong during the test," I say.

"Sims promised!" Peace yells. "He said nothing would happen."

"I'm sorry," I say. "But I think Mr. Sims fucked you over. And Brian."

Hearing Brian's name infuriates Peace.

He paces back and forth about a foot off the hospital room floor. Now a new nurse has arrived. She pulls gown open on Peace's chest, clasps her hands together and begins CPR compressions.

"Look," I say, hope in my voice, "They're trying to revive you, to bring you back to life."

Then an insane idea occurs to me.

"Listen to me. Can you, Peace? Listen? Right now," I'm serious now, grim. "There's not much time."

Peace nods but I can tell he is confused.

"Peace," I say, desperate now. "I don't have time to explain. But I need you to listen carefully to what I'm going to say and to remember. All of it."

Peace listens.

"I think Sims is running some sort of medical billing scam. I'm not sure how it works, but I think he convinced Brian to fake chest pains, just like you.

Peace looks at me, suspicious now. "How do you know about that?"

"I can't explain now. I'm sorry. I think Sims is working with a man at this hospital. His name is Nilsson. N-I-L-S-S-O-N. 22282 Circle Drive, Carthay Circle. 22282! "

Peace's expression clouds and I realize that he has no idea what I am talking about.

Shit. Another nurse removes the mask from Peace's face and pushes a tube attached to a plastic breathing bag into his mouth, then begins to squeeze it rhythmically.

"Peace!" I yell. "You must come with me and the dog right now, please! I'm begging you!"

Chapter 73

> *"I didn't want any flowers, I only wanted*
> *To lie with my hands turned up and be utterly empty. How free it is,*
> *you have no idea how free——*
> *The peacefulness is so big it dazes you,*
> *And it asks nothing, a name tag, a few trinkets.It is what the dead*
> *close on, finally; I imagine them*
> *Shutting their mouths on it, like a Communion tablet."*
> *Sylvia Plath*

The rain falls in black torrents, submerging the sidewalk outside Nilsson's house and washing away his lawn. Rose is the first one to pass through the locked wrought iron gate, then Peace, who hesitates at first, and then I follow him through. We sail quickly past the drowning ficus trees and the almost-overflowing pool to the area in the back, then through the low wooden fence.

When Peace sees the dog, he moans.

The dog is still tied with rope to the metal pole, its ribcage visible under the wet fur, matted with mud. The water bowl overflows with dirty rainwater, but there is no food and the dog shivers violently in the cold. Turds slowly disintegrate around him in the rain.

I look at Peace. "The monster who did this is a friend of Mr. Sims. All you have to do—if you live—is to remember the address here and make sure someone calls the police right away. 22282 Circle—"

Rose's crazy barking interrupts me. She's jumping up and down, then scratching the wet ground right next to the dog.

"Rose," I say, as if she can understand me, "Quiet. This man will help the dog if you are quiet."

But Rose won't stop. She's going nuts, barking, jumping and, running around the dog.

"She wants to show you something," Peace says.

"I thought you were afraid of dogs," I say, but move closer to Rose, just to see if I can calm her down.

"Dogs are trained to hate black people," Peace says. "But your dog seems okay."

As soon as we approach, Rose gives me a serious look, then sinks, rear paws first, into the cold wet ground right under the suffering dog. We watch her as she disappears. What the fuck?

"Where'd she go?"

"I don't know," I say, and wait for Rose to rise up again from the mud.

Chapter 74

> *"I know death hath ten thousand several doors*
> *For me to take their exit."*
> John Webster, Duchess of Malfi

The tethered dog trembles and the rain comes down.

Peace and I stand staring at the ground where Rose just was. "Maybe you should go find her," he says.

He's right. Any second now the pressure being applied to the heart inside that body on the hospital bed will startle the muscle back to life, and the lungs, forced full of air, will breathe on their own. And there will go my only chance to save the dog.

"You have to come, too," I say. I can't risk losing him now. Peace nods, realizing, I think, that not much more can go wrong for him now.

We sink below the ground facing one another, a dead fat white man and a dead naked black man, as if we're riding in an express elevator to the netherworld.

Down we sink through the black wet earth, through a network of gnarled dead roots, through rocks and shards of glass, through slugs, chicken bones and colonies of worms. About three feet below the surface I see Rose waiting beside a transparent plastic storage box, the kind people store sweaters in to keep the moths away. She is overjoyed to see me, and licks my face, then licks Peace's foot.

The box has been wrapped in plastic, but without my glasses and because it's so dark down here, all I can make out are small grayish packages piled one upon another.

"What's inside?" I ask and Peace peers into the side of the plastic box.

"Shit," he says.

"What do you see?" I ask.

"They're bundles of bills," Peace says as he disappears, "A shitload of money."

Chapter 75

> *"I hope the leaving is joyful; and I hope never to return."*
> Frida Kahlo

Peace is back on the Cath lab bed, which shakes under the pressure of the CPR compressions he's receiving on his chest. The mask lies next to his head. A breathing bag is in his mouth now, and a nurse is squeezing it.

Rose stays close to him, so close that he'd feel her warm breath on his cheek—if he could feel anything and she had breath.

"80 systolic," a nurse shouts.

"Stop CPR." The doctor says.

No! Don't stop! Don't give up! Don't give up now!

But the nurse stops the compressions on his chest and stands back from the bed. Then the breathing bag is removed from Peace's mouth.

Peace lies there, eyes closed, his bare chest exposed. Is it rising and falling?

"We have a pulse."

Chapter 76

> *"If I die, where does Time go?"*
> Sean Jones, *"Esperanto"*

We stay with Peace in the Cath Lab, then in the ICU, where he's given an EKG and connected to monitors and to a fresh IV. His eyes sometimes flutter open, and from what I hear the nurses say, he should recover quickly and fully from his rare reaction to the angiographic dye.

But Peace doesn't seem fine at all. He hasn't spoken. Not even a grunt. Not even a murmur. And the longer he's silent, the closer that dog comes to death.

Will Peace remember what happened? What he remember what he saw? Me? Rose? The dog? The buried stash of money? Me? Rose? Or does a return from death to life require the survivor to relinquish his special knowledge to forgetfulness?

Rose floats above his bed; I keep close to the electronic monitor. A nurse I haven't seen before—a tall, graceful African American woman in her fifties with short gray hair and red-framed glasses—enters the glass cubicle and touches Peace's hand. "Mr. Peace? I'm Diane. I'll be around for the next twelve hours. Are you awake?"

Peace opens his eyes. Diane smiles. "You must feel pretty drowsy from all the meds they gave you," she smiles, and checks his IV. "I hear you had a pretty wild night."

Peace seems to hear her. The pupils in his dilated eyes contract. "Where am I?" he asks thickly.

"You're in the Memorial Medical Center ICU," Diane says cheerfully. "You had a little problem during your angiogram, but you're fine now. The doctors just want to keep a close watch on you for the next 12 or 14 hours."

Peace frowns and shakes his head. "Is it still raining? Or did I dream that?"

"Oh, it's raining all right," Diane says. "Some of the 405 is flooded, now. And it's freezing. Absolutely freezing." Peace strains to sit up, but Diane gently stops him. "Take it easy, Mr. Peace. We don't want you to pull out your IV or get dizzy. You've been through a lot."

"I died." Peace says flatly, as if he's only now remembering. "I was dead."

Diane tilts her head and smiles. "I wouldn't say that, exactly, but for a few minutes, yes, you came awfully close." Diane changes the subject, "Are you thirsty? Would you like some water or some ice chips? The doctor wants to start you on liquids first. "

Peace frowns, as if he's making a difficult calculation in his head. "I need to talk to a policeman."

Diane's slender brows furrow. "Well, right now, Mr. Peace, the best thing for you is to close your eyes and rest."

"Peace says, his voice clearer now, and stronger. "I need to talk to the police. Right now. Right here. Please, can you call them for me? Or is there a phone in here so I can dial 9-1-1 myself?

Diane keeps smiling but pushes a small button on the monitor, then nods to a nurse in the station beyond through the glass. "I think you had a nightmare, Mr. Peace," she says. "You're safe now. There's no need to call the police."

Peace looks directly at Diane, "I'm sober. I saw a policeman when I was in the ER. Can you call him? I need to talk to him. There's a life at stake!"

The other nurse has entered the small cubicle and exchanges a look with Diane. She leans over Peace and says, "How are you doing, Mr. Peace?" I'm Joy, the head ICU nurse."

Leave him the fuck alone, I think. Listen to him. Listen!

155

"Call the police!" Peace shouts, agitated now and trying to get out of the narrow bed.

Diane talks quietly to Joy, "I think Mr. Peace is hallucinating from the drug cocktail he got in the Cath Lab."

"I'm cold sober." Peace asserts. "I'm not seeing things. I need to talk to the police about a crime. A crime in progress. Will you help me do that? Please!"

"I'm sorry," Joy scolds. "We can't do that. And you'll have to calm down. If you cause a disturbance, there will be consequences."

Peace looks wildly around the little cubicle, then rips the IV out of his arm. Droplets of his blood trickle on the white sheet as he pushes over the IV pole and hoists himself over the side rails of the high hospital bed.

"Stop!" Joy yells.

"Don't do this, Mr. Peace" Diane entreats.

Peace pushes the women aside and bounds out of the small cubicle, then barefoot and naked under his hospital gown, scans the hallway. Rose and I are with him when he runs a to a glass fire alarm box near the elevators. Peace makes a fist and breaks the glass, cutting his hand.

Peace pulls the red FIRE lever with his bloody hand just before two uniformed police officers grab him and roughly throw him down.

Chapter 77

> *"Death's truer name*
> *Is "Onward..."*
> *Tennyson*

The hospital's electronic fire alarm is so deafening and powerful that the walls seem to pulsate with the sound. Frightened and angry patients in bathrobes and fuzzy socks stand outside their rooms or struggle toward the elevator. Janitors, orderlies, and men and women in scrubs, along with two security guards, rush back and forth.

Rose hovers close to what we can see of Peace, just the pink undersides of his bare feet, sticking out from below a tangle of police officers. Joy and Diane wave at a man in dress slacks and a dress shirt who emerges breathless from the stairwell and who carries a serious looking ring of keys. He pushes past the knot of people and inserts one of the keys into a slot inside the alarm box, restoring silence. Then, just when my dead ears are adjusting to the quiet, a male voice booms from PA system: "FALSE ALARM! FALSE ALARM! THERE IS NO FIRE. REPEAT. FALSE ALARM. Ambulatory patients, please return immediately to your rooms. If you need assistance, please stay where you are. Hospital staff, returns to your workstations."

The police officers are upright now and one of them roughly handcuffs Peace. I think his nose is broken from having been pushed flat on his face. Blood runs from his arm and from his mouth—did he bite his tongue or break a tooth? Rose is barking, whining, crying.

"You are under arrest," a heavy woman officer says and pushes Peace roughly back toward the ICU. "You have the right to remain silent. Anything you say can and will be used against you in a court of law. You have the right to an attorney. If you cannot afford an attorney, one will be provided for you. Do you understand the rights I have just read to you? With these rights in mind, do you wish to speak to me?"

I want to hold my breath, but don't have any.

"Yes. Yes. I want to speak with you." Peace says thickly. "I want to speak with you all right now."

Chapter 78

"Nothing can happen more beautiful than death."
Walt Whitman

Joy and Diane secure Peace to his ICU bed with wide black Velcro restraints, reinsert his IV, and put a latex glove filled with ice cubes on his swollen nose. His teeth are intact, they say, he's only bitten the inside of his cheek. They seem disappointed at this news, but cheer up when they inform Peace that as soon as they get his discharge from the ICU, he will be transferred to the jail ward over at County.

Rose and I silently urge him on— and float—like those faint galaxies in deep space—over Peace as he gives his statement to the police, one officer standing at the foot of his bed, the other sitting to the side. What Peace tells them is strange and sad, but despite his swollen mouth, he speaks with conviction and with clarity—about a suffering dog forced to stand guard over a plastic box of money—about Wings of Hope and a man named Sims, and about his friend Brian, who shouldn't have died.

Peace stops speaking, then waits expectantly, looking first at the male policeman by the bed, then to the other, the woman. "Make the call now," he says simply. "Please."

The female officer looks questioningly at her partner. He shrugs, then nods. She removes the portable radio from her belt and quickly punches in a number. "Animal Control? This is LAPD Officer Brown over at MMC hospital. Yes, I have an emergency, a dog in extreme distress at 2282 Circle Drive, Carthay Circle. I repeat, extreme distress. The owner of the residence, a Mr. Nilsson, may be a case of felony animal abuse."

Chapter 79

> *"I am become Death, the Shatterer of Worlds."*
> The Bhagavad Gita

It is still dark when the white Animal Control truck pulls up on Circle Drive. The rain comes down in heavy swirling sheets. Two animal control officers get out of the vehicle, both wearing long, plastic ponchos over their dark uniforms. One carries a powerful flashlight, the other a white pole with some kind of leash attached.

One of them knocks on Nilsson's front door sharply, then rings the bell and waits. Nothing. They turn and walk carefully through the slippery mud to the iron gate—it's locked. The tall officer kneels, then the other one, a woman, steps onto his cupped hands so he can hoist her over. Once on the other side, the woman reaches for the long pole. The tall man stays outside the gate sweeping the backyard behind it with his flashlight's beam.

Rose and I and the woman follow the light to the low fence in the back.   Will she keep going? Will she even look? Or will she stop now and turn back?

Her head down, the female officer moves to the low brown fence and then behind it, pointing the white pole in front of her like a weapon. But when she sees the dog, lying on its side now in the mud and water, she lets the pole go and drops down to her knees beside it.

Chapter 80

> *"Jazz isn't dead. It just smells funny."*
> Frank Zappa

What Rose and I saw afterwards:

The rope was cut and the dog rescued. The pair of Animal control officers rushed it to a 24-hour vet over on Olympic Blvd. There it received IV fluids and nourishment, was wrapped in blankets and was placed on a heating pad.

The dog is male, approximately 6 months old, a lab and Spaniel mix. A mutt.

Soon two police cars arrived on Circle Drive. One of the officers took two shovels out of his car's trunk. The other had a camera. The officers from the other car went to the front door with a search warrant.

The heavy rain had loosened the hard topsoil, but it still took two hours of digging to unearth the shrink-wrapped plastic box. Inside, the officers estimated, was almost 7 million dollars, some in cash and some in certificates of deposit in Nilsson's name.

Outside Wings of Hope, two police officers led Sims in handcuffs, his leather jacket covering his head, into a black and white.

The time Peace spent in the County hospital jail ward was brief and not too bad. The story of the dog and the medical billing scam —how Nilsson paid Sims to provide fake patients, who then received unnecessary and expensive tests that brought in millions of dollars from Medicare and Medicaid—was big news. A lawyer from the D.A.'s office visited Peace and offered him a deal—all charges against him dropped in exchange for his testimony against Sims.

The money in the buried box? Cash that Nilsson, the hospital CFO, had skimmed from Medicare payments for padded billings for the fake patients Sims had sent him.

Chapter 81

"We never become really and genuinely our entire and honest selves until we are dead —and not then until we have been dead years and years. People ought to start dead and then they would be honest so much earlier."
Mark Twain

Rose glides along the grassy slope—well, not actually on it, but she skims its gentle contour, an inch or so above the tips of the sharp, bright blades. Down. Then up. Then down. It's a weird game, but for Rose this place offers grass uninterrupted, therefore grass perfected, as close to a heavenly meadow as she will ever come. Since her paws can't touch or feel the surface, the curving rows of rectangular bronze markers pressed into the earth cannot impede her graceful progress. Nor can she know that each bears one name among the infinity of names belonging to the dead.

Today is the unveiling, the coming out party for the marker on my grave. It's been almost a year since I died on Gower Street, almost a year since Rose has visited this place. I was reluctant to return, but the grass sold me. The only other occasion we've had for visiting the living world, there was grass, too— a front lawn in Pasadena bordered by mature jacaranda trees. Maybe it was May. The tree's blossoms clustered in thick clouds of purple. A black dog ran back and forth chasing a red ball in the grass below, a few bright petals stuck to his gleaming fur.

Rose did not do what I thought she would—fly to the dog, then prance with joy in the air around him and try to lick his face. She held back and studied the scene before her, her eyes intense as they followed the dog's movements.

The dog was much bigger—his forehead wide and his body filled-out and muscular. He wore a green, red and black plaid collar and his eyes were bright. A little girl, twelve maybe, stroked his head when he dropped the ball at her feet. The dog licked her face.

"Good job, Jimmy!" the girl said. "Good job!"

Rose looked away.

Then she turned to me as if to say, I'm finished here. It took a moment, but I think I understood then what Rose had seen—not just the dog—safe now, healthy, loved—but how much she had been denied in life and how great her suffering had been.

Rose keeps up her solitary game above the hill. I drift slowly to my burial site. A blue velvet cloth covers the memorial plaque, and a dozen or so white chairs, the kind caterers use, have been arranged in rows. There's also a microphone connected to a portable generator, as well as lights and reflectors.

Now I see a red and white KNWS van parked at the bottom of the hill, right next to my shit brother Mark's Ferrari.

Mark is thinner and, if this is even possible, his step seems more buoyant. He wears a black suit that shines a little in the sunlight, and under the jacket I see a black t-shirt. Now he's a fucking hipster? Some of the others who were here to see me buried have returned—My sociopathic former business partner Joshua Kay—(Why did he come? Because he's a fucking sociopath.)—and Trinka, his bitch wife, look wonderful.

My shit brother Mark I already mentioned. Helen, his wife and decorator, looks almost too good. Did she get her nose done? Her ass? Her chin? Margarita, my cleaning lady is here with her son. He's grown tall and angular and has the beginning of a beard.

Absent are my cousin Sheila, my former wives, their boyfriends and the parasites; also my accountant, my barber, Tony, Lena, the office manager, and my neighbor from my shit apartment on Cahuenga. Julia, Mark says to someone, is unfortunately in Europe on a wine-tasting trip.

I thought I saw two lean canine shadows darting across the road at the bottom of the hill. Were these the two coyotes? I'm not sure.　　Mark and Helen, whose high heels sink into the porous surface with each step, talks now with an overly-made up woman who must be a television reporter. Then I recognize her. What is she doing here? When I died she was just the weather girl, popular for her too-tight sweaters and Valley Girl diction. Now she wears a brown business suit and flats.

The rabbi appears, the same dumpy woman as before—she must be part of some package deal—and after a short schmooze with Mark, the living sit down and she recites, in English, the 23rd Psalm.

I remain vertical, ambivalent, not wanting to be present——or to hear these living voices or to see these faces.

The Lord is my shepherd, I shall not want.
He makes me lie down in green pastures.

I watch Rose frolic above her own weird version of pasture, admiring how her paws move through the air. He leads me beside still waters; he restores my soul.

Then the dumpy rabbi delivers a brief eulogy—Charles Stone did such and such, liked this and that, worked here and there.

The unveiling of the marker is like looking at myself in one of those trick carnival mirrors—it's me all right, but terribly distorted:

CHARLES STONE
1984-2012
Always In Our Hearts

Whose fucking hearts? I wonder. I guess they couldn't have it say,

"Disappointing Son. Pain in the Ass Brother. Failed Husband. Indifferent Stepfather. Fuck Him."

The Rabbi then petitions the Creator to grant my soul true rest upon the wings of the divine presence. For, as the Rabbi explains, Charles has gone to that other world—which at this moment I am almost homesick for.

After the Rabbi reads the Kaddish, I think it's over. But my shit brother Mark bounces up, and nods to the reporter. A guy in jeans appears from the van and turns on the hot white lights, then angles the reflectors. Here comes the cameraman, the heavy video camera on his shoulder. And a makeup woman, who dusts the reporter's, then Mark's, faces with powder.

Mark bounces over to the microphone, but waits to speak until the TV woman nods again.

"Everyone," he says. "Thank you for coming today. Today is not important just because it is the anniversary of my brother's death, but because until today, his murderer has gone free. Until today, the Stone family has not been able to have closure."

Closure? I've been dead for a year.

Mark continues, "I want to share with you some sad but important news. You may remember that about four weeks ago, a forty-two year old man named Bradley Roth died after being hit by a car while he was riding his bicycle on Santa Monica Boulevard. Some of you may remember that Bradley Roth was a screenwriter who wrote for the very successful 'Wild and Free' movie series."

Where the fuck is this going? I'm sorry this guy died, but those movies were crap.

"Mr. Roth was wearing a fanny pack when he died. In it officers found a .32 caliber pistol. Ballistics tests have revealed that the bullets removed from my brother's body match Mr. Roth's gun exactly."

Wait. This asshole screenwriter is the one who killed me? A fucking asshole bicyclist screenwriter shot me because I yelled at him for hogging the road?

"—Now I'd like to talk about the disposition of the reward."

What was I expecting? Mr. Moriarity on a bicycle? And a fanny pack, yet? Why not a man purse?

Now Helen has joined Mark at the microphone, her sharp heels sinking now through the moist grass to the earth below. "As you might remember, AndyCo. and its partner MultiCorp joined together last year to offer a reward to anyone with information about my brother's murder. Rather than just withdraw the money now, the family, AndyCo. and Multicorp want to do something meaningful that will honor my brother's memory and prevent senseless deaths like his." Shut up! Just shut up, I think. Honor my memory, my ass. You know what would be fucking meaningful? If you would just shut the fuck up.

But Mark continues talking, "So we have decided donate the $50,000 reward—and our ongoing financial support—to the LAPD's anti-gang youth program GangStoppers, for the development of a new outreach project targeting tweens. This project will be called Charlie's Kids in memory of my late brother, Charles Stone. The family and AndyCo. hope that—"

I can't listen to another fucking word. I can't bear my shit brother's voice. His suit. His wife. His black t-shirt. Leave it to him to find the public relations possibilities in my murder —not once— twice.

And tweens? Who even thought of such a term? But it's clever: Now AndyCo. will sell some cheese balls, too.

Well, shit brother Mark, you've won. Yippee and Howdy-do. I concede defeat.

Mark's speech over, he receives the admiration and gratitude of the assembled. Then, with my gravesite as backdrop, the TV woman records commentary for the evening news. I look away from them and turn toward

Rose—thin, graceful, almost birdlike above the expanse of living green.

Rose changes direction and flies toward me.

When she reaches me, she tries to lick my face, then tries to press her slender body against mine. I can't feel her here, but I know well the sensation of her rough dry tongue against my face and the light pressure of her slim body against my chest.

I pat her silky head and smile into her wise brown eyes. She wags her tail.

"Rose," I say, "Sweet Rosie. Let's go. Let's go home. "

THE END

Charlie & Rose continue their adventures in Dead Is Best - out now from Fahrenheit Press...

Chapter 1

"Most of the people I admire . . . are either dead or not feeling well."
Tom Waits

The girl wasn't with us and then she was. I could say that she appeared suddenly or like a bat out of hell—but neither evokes the gloomy precipitousness of her arrival.

I was combing the reddish fur on Rose's back with my fingers—then scratching the places behind her ears that she likes scratched—and trying to fully occupy the seamless, boundless Sabbath that is death—at least mine and Rose's.

Then here she is in the middle of our perpetual nowhere looking awful.

She's dressed in black leather leggings and a silvery sleeveless top. Her brown hair has been bleached corn silk yellow and straightened into perfect verticality. But she's blue around the edges—as if she'd dipped her fingers and toes in grape juice—bluish toes and toenails of her pale bare feet, blue lips, and blue-edged nostrils. Her pupils are tiny black pinholes in the glacier-blue of her irises and her thick black eyeliner and mascara just make them seem blacker.

You'd think in death Rose and I would have some fucking privacy. You'd think that having given up the ghost I'd be beyond the grasp of my ex-stepdaughter, the parasite.

Chapter 2

> *"The dead are way more organized than the living."*
> China Mieville

Her name is Cali. Cali Green. She was fifteen the last time I saw her—which was at my funeral—during which she was busy texting or applying makeup. That was almost two years ago, more or less—time doesn't exist here. When I was briefly and unfortunately married to her mother, her name was—get this—Cali Green Stone. I'm Stone. Charles Stone. But people always pronounced the last two names as one—Greenstone.

A stupid hippie name like Cali Green Stone might have been a problem for her, but at her fancy schmancy progressive, exclusive, private college preparatory school off Mulholland Drive, that's the kind of name kids had. The parents—oral surgeons and architects and screenwriters and actors and movie directors and rock musicians—were Sallys and Ruths, Steves and Michaels. Yet behold their offspring––Truth, Canyon, Druid, Turquoise, Vanilla and Road. Don't tell me those are names—they're brands.

Those pretentious, fucked-up names are why I decided to name Rose "Rose." "Rose" is beautiful, evocative, delicate, and feminine in a sweet old-fashioned way. And Rose is all these things fully and without irony—perhaps because Rose is a dead dog—and because of all she learned about suffering during her short life.

But Cali—please—tell me what fucking kind of name is that for human being— even one from L.A.?

What was her mother thinking when she chose that name? But the less I think about what her mother—my ex-wife number three—thought or thinks the better. One thing I'm sure of though, she wasn't contemplating Kali, the dark Hindu goddess of undoing when she named her daughter.

My ex-wife wouldn't know Kali if the goddess kicked her bony ass with her bare blue foot.

Cali's pupils fix me in their gaze, and then constrict into the impossible blue paleness of her eyes. "Charles," she screams, her bluish hand reaching for me. "Charles, help me!"

Dead Is Best by Jo Perry is out now from Fahrenheit Press

Printed in Great Britain
by Amazon